SUICIDE MOST FOUL

J. G. Jeffreys

Suicide
Most Foul

WALKER AND COMPANY
NEW YORK

First published in the United States of America
in 1981 by the Walker Publishing Company, Inc.

ISBN: 0-8027-5430-9

Library of Congress Catalog Card Number: 80-52078

Printed in the United States of America

10 9 8 7 6 5 4 3 2 1

Editor's Note

There is no reference to Sturrock in any of the very numerous memoirs and letters relating to the Waterloo campaign. In view of the curious story he has to tell here, this is hardly surprising; but there is no doubt that he was actually present from his account of several details. The little known fact, for instance, that Wellington's brilliant Quartermaster-General, Colonel Sir William de Lancey, was an American; the comparatively modest nature of the Duchess of Richmond's ballroom instead of the glittering palace which is usually described; the reference to disaffected elements of the Allied troops firing on Wellington; the impediment of sodden, shoulder-high barley and rye on the battlefield, etc.

On the other hand, he seems to have got the timing of the battle itself wrong. The first French infantry march of d'Erlon's divisions, followed by the undisciplined and near-disastrous British cavalry counter-charge, came shortly after two o'clock in the afternoon; while the series of hideously wasteful French cavalry attacks did not start until about an hour later. Similarly, Bonaparte's 'Proclamation' was found in or near his abandoned carriage after the rout—although copies of it might certainly have been sent to London beforehand by British agents in Paris—and Wellington's remark, "Napoleon has humbugged me, by God," was actually made in the Duke of Richmond's private study. But one can allow Sturrock these minor inaccuracies for the sake of his story.

B.J.H.

There was a sound of revelry by night,
And Belgium's capital had gather'd then
Her Beauty and her Chivalry, and bright
The lamps shone o'er fair women and brave men;
A thousand hearts beat happily; and when
Music arose with its voluptuous swell,
Soft eyes look'd love to eyes which spake again,
And all went merry as a marriage bell;
But hush! Hark! a deep sound strikes like a rising knell!

Did ye not hear it—No; 'twas but the wind,
Or the car rattling o'er the stony street;
On with the dance! let joy be unconfined;
No sleep till morn, when Youth and Pleasure meet
To chase the glowing Hours with flying feet—
But hark!—that heavy sound breaks in once more,
As if the clouds its echo would repeat;
And nearer, clearer, deadlier than before!
Arm! Arm! it is—it is—the cannon's opening roar!

And there was mounting in hot haste: the steed,
The mustering squadron, and the clattering car,
Went pouring forward with impetuous speed,
And swiftly forming in the ranks of war;
And the deep thunder peal on peal afar;
And near, the beat of the alarming drum
Roused up the soldier ere the morning star;
While throng'd the citizens with terror dumb,
Or whispering, with white lips—'The foe! they come! they come!'

'The Eve of Waterloo'
Childe Harold's Pilgrimage
LORD BYRON

One

I consider it a mere commonplace of genteel manners that a man who takes a whim to blow his brains out with a pistol firing a one-ounce ball should do it in his own lodgings. To perform the act in the residence of an amiable and titled lady shows no consideration for the servants, and little respect for a fine Aubusson carpet. But such was the opening of the vexatious affair that took me, my groom Jagger and my horrible little clerk, Master Maggsy, to the great Battle of Waterloo in that fateful June of 1815. There we witnessed the final cooking of that rascal Bonaparte's tripes for him, and had sundry curious dealings with several of the Duke of Wellington's troops; the infamous army, as he called it. 'I don't know what they'll do to the French,' he said, 'but, by God, they frighten me.'

So for the start of it you are to see me with one or two military gentlemen, and several others of Philosophy and learning, etc., at the town house of Lady Dorothea Dash-wood—Lady Dorothea Hookham as was—in Hanover Square. It is the occasion of her weekly salon, my lady being somewhat of the blue-stocking persuasion, and we are gathered in the Adams drawing-room, discoursing over our dishes of tea; a niminy-piminy beverage I can well do without, though I take it politely enough when in genteel company. The ladies present are Lady Dorothea herself, her companion and duenna Miss Harriet Hookham, a particular sharp and shrewd old female much resembling an ancient grey parrot, and a pert and pretty chit not above eighteen years old; by name Miss Georgina Wilde-Hookham and, as I understand, a country cousin of my lady's up to Town to learn the ways of London. And by the look of her, and the way she is studying a certain young captain of Hussars also present, there is not a lot she don't already know.

In short, a very proper company and I take a reasonable pride in finding myself admitted to it. But I have said enough of my own humble beginnings in several other of my remarkable works, and shall say no more here, except to add that I am rightly considered to be the ornament of the Bow Street police force—the Runners, as they are still called— the first exponent of the Art and Science of Detection, and an officer very far removed from your common thief-taker. All in all, a temptation to the ladies, though I have never yet succumbed to the bliss of matrimony, having a sound investment or two, a comfortable account with Mr Coutts' Bank, and my own chaise and horses with a groom and stable-boy to look after them in the mews behind my lodgings in Soho Square; these being above Mrs Spilsbury's well-known Medical Parlour and Dispensary. Nevertheless, a modest man with it all.

There I was then sitting with my dish of tea and, to tell the truth, reflecting on the several attractions of a certain young red-headed French lady—with whom I had been studying the intricacies of the language and various other complexities for some time past—rather than paying much attention to the polite conversation about me. It was the innocent seeming little country miss that had put me in mind of Juliette, for there is no mistaking that look about 'em, and I was not surprised when she rolled her speaking dark blue eyes at the captain of Hussars and enquired, 'When do you leave for Brussels, Captain ffoulkes? Or do you think to sit the war out here in London?'

Had I been the captain the little tit would have found herself across my knee with her petticoats upped and her arse spanked, genteel company or not, but the gallant young gentleman merely flushed as pink as his pantaloons and protested, 'Why, no indeed, Miss Georgina. I'm only waiting for my horses. The guv'nor's sending 'em up from the country for me, and when they come I'm hotfoot for the Harwich packet. Most likely tomorrow. I don't mean to be late for the fun.'

My lady is not by no means the handsomest woman in London, but she has the kindest of natures; none the less in spite of some of her crackpot notions she can be uncommon sharp when she pleases. It was not in her to see a brave young fellow so put down, but neither was it in her innocence to perceive that some sort of brief message had passed between the pair of 'em, for she said, 'Come now, miss. That was too pert. I'll have you ask Captain ffoulkes' pardon for it.'

The chit rolled her eyes down as demure as she'd rolled 'em round naughty. 'To be sure I will, Cousin Dorothea,' she announced. 'A thousand of the prettiest pardons. To-morrow is it, Captain ffoulkes? How I wish I were a man myself to ride out to halt the Corsican Monster.'

There's mischief brewing here, I thought softly to myself, and Miss Harriet sniffed; an expression the clever old lady uses for many a song without words. But, seemingly innocent, Lady Dorothea continued, 'It all seems quiet enough yet, though not for much longer, I fear. I met Catherine Saltoun in the Park yesterday and she has lately had word from Lord Alexander, who is Lieutenant-Colonel of the First Foot Guards. He observed that for some time past the Duke of Wellington has been riding a great deal, adding how they used to say in Spain that when the Beau went riding it was time to look out. Otherwise he says all is quite gay at Enghien. The officers and men are mostly playing cricket.' She smiled somewhat sadly at the young Hussar, adding, 'You'll not be late for it, Captain ffoulkes, though whether it may be fun or not is another matter. What do you make of the situation, Mr Sturrock?' she asked me.

'Why, very simple, ma'am,' I answered. 'There'll be more than cricket balls flying before long. The correspondent of *The Times* says that along with the Prussians we're holding a line very near a hundred miles long, and Bonaparte only has to breach it at one point to make himself master of Europe again. The rascal needs but one quick victory, and he'll fling all he has in to get it."

'Oh,' says Miss Pert sweetly, joining in again unasked, 'but Bonaparte will not break the line.' She took the roving eye away from Captain ffoulkes's mustachios and fixed it on me. 'It's plain he'll advance on Brussels, and if General Prince Blücher don't hold him before, the Duke means to stop him close by a place called Waterloo. It seems there's a ridge of high ground, just south of Brussels, and that's where Wellington will stand,' Miss Georgina explained kindly to me. 'That's why he's been riding out so much of late. To survey his dispositions.'

I gazed at the prodigy goggle-mouthed, as did another

military gentleman sitting close by; a grizzled and teak-faced fellow in his middle forties and an unfamiliar uniform, bearing the insignia of a major. 'Well, miss,' he said, when he got his breath back, 'That's fine and uncommon knowledge. Where did you . . .?'

But before he could finish there was another and yet more startling distraction. A sudden and sharp spitting bang seeming to come from the hall. It crashed like a cannon, and at once all was confusion; tea dishes let slip, exclamations, the chit screaming, Miss Harriet demanding, 'What the devil?' and my lady crying, 'What of heaven's name was that?'

'That, ma'am,' I announced briefly, 'was a pistol shot,' and was halfway to the door as I spoke.

But before I could reach so far it was flung open in my face to reveal Lady Dorothea's ancient and most respectable butler, Mr Masters, as white as chalk and gobbling like a ghost, opening and shutting his trap but getting never a sensible word out. What was worse, the old gentleman was clinging to the door in his agitation, blocking my way to the hall, preventing any sight of what might be about there, and fresh cries and confusion as the ladies rushed to his assistance. It was near enough a full minute before I got out myself, with the major and Captain ffoulkes and some of the other gentlemen after me.

The hall was proper and commodious as befits a fashionable town house; black and white marble floor and elegant pillars, a fair bit of naked statuary in the Italian manner, a curving staircase with a wrought-iron and gilt handrail, and several doors. To our left the main entrance on the square, one to the servants' quarters under the stairs, one more to a morning room at the back of the house, another opposite to us. These would be the most important, I concluded in an instant's survey, and there was nothing untoward in the hall itself; save that the door opposite was half open, with a wreath of gunpowder smoke hanging out of it in the air.

Of the horrid scene in the small room beyond I shall say little, except to observe that the carpet would never be the same again. The gentleman lying there—for so he appeared to be from his faded and somewhat shabby but carefully tended clothes—had had the top of his head taken off by a pistol ball fired seemingly at point blank; while the weapon, still warm, was also lying close by his right hand. And if the fellow had performed the rash act himself, as at present it seemed, he had made a very fair job of it.

All this I took in on the instant, and by now there was some considerable confusion behind, what with Miss Harriet snapping out orders to the servants, Lady Dorothea calling for one of 'em to fetch a physician for Mr Masters, Miss Georgina chattering like a jay, and a press of gentlemen at my back with the major and Captain ffoulkes in the forefront gazing at the corpse; the captain of an uncommon greenish shade of countenance which ill-matched the colour of his pantaloons. It wanted only my little monster, Master Maggsy, to make the scene complete, and sure he appeared, for he has a nose like a hound for blood and mischief, and close beside him Miss Georgina.

'God's whiskers,' the wretch started but whatever else he added was lost in a shriek from the chit that might have broke the windows as she caught sight of what was on the floor. Whereupon she swooned into the willing arms of Captain ffoulkes, and I lost my own patience. 'Get her out of it,' I cried, 'and likewise keep the other ladies out. And all the rest of you retire; though nobody's to leave the house until I give the word. We've a vexatious mishap here, and it may be a Bow Street matter.' But I paused with the major, for he was looking down at the corpse with an expression as if he knew the man, and he seemed more commonsensical about it than the rest of 'em. To him I said, 'All save yourself, sir. I'll be obliged if you'll remain for a word or two.' He nodded briefly, and I then added to Maggsy, 'And you can get about your own business, my lad.'

Maggsy has his uses, and he understood what I meant by that. He also nodded, with his wicked grin, and disappeared like the imp he is. So we were left alone in quiet with the door closed on us, and the major observed, 'The young captain took it ill. Teacup soldier, is he? He'll see worse before this month's out.'

'No doubt,' I agreed. 'As no doubt you've seen worse yourself.'

He noded once more. 'So, so. India and the Peninsula. It looks different on the field, though, And this is damned odd.'

'Oddity is its first feature,' I said. 'In several respects. Permit me to make myself known. Sturrock of Bow Street. And you, sir?'

'Finchingfield,' he announced. 'Major. Attached to the staff of the Quartermaster-General; Colonel Sir William de Lancey.'

'I'm obliged, sir,' I told him. 'I noted the way you looked at this man. Do you recognise him?'

'Ain't a lot left to recognise, is there?' he asked. 'I know who he is, if that's what you mean. Captain Louis Fénelon. Commanding a squadron of Boney's Twelfth Chasseurs at one time.'

'What?' I demanded. 'A Frenchman?'

'Wouldn't find much else in that lot, would you?' he

enquired reasonably. 'Poor devil was in the retreat from Moscow. Lost most of his squadron at Smolensk, and the rest of 'em at the crossing of the Berezina. Then, when Boney himself left his army in the lurch and bolted for Paris soon after, he deserted. Wasn't the only one neither.'

'A deserter *and* a Frenchy,' I cried. 'By God, that makes a fine confection. So what the devil is he doing here? And how do you know so much about him, sir?'

The major gave me a singular curious, sly look. 'As to the first, I fancy her ladyship might explain more than I can. For the second, the man told me himself. What's more to the point for now is did he do that, or was it done for him?'

'If it was done for him,' I said, 'the hand responsible must have made a damned quick escape. There are only three doors he could have got out by. The one to the square, the other to the morning room and garden, and the last through the servants' quarters. We shall soon discover if anybody saw the fellow; if he exists. I've already set my clerk on that inquiry, and he's a sharp little rascal. But it's plain that Mr Masters, the butler, is our prime source. I mean to question him myself as soon as the commotion dies down. You'll understand that it's best to tread lightly in a household of this kind.'

'Aye,' he murmured, half to himself, 'I can see it is. But I'd say there wasn't time for another man to escape,' he continued. 'Little more than a minute from the bang to when we got here. And at his age the very look of this lot'd be enough to frighten the other old fellow into fits if he happened to catch sight of it. Hears the shot, pokes his head round the door to see what's amiss, and there you have it. From what little I know of 'em the nearest upper servants ever get to see the colour of blood is port wine.'

'Very likely,' I agreed somewhat absently, turning to survey the chamber itself though there was little enough in it to study. In was a little ante-room in which the lesser sort of visitors are placed while waiting to be received; very likely those for Lady Dorothea's husband, Mr Dashwood, he being a Member of Parliament and no doubt often having clients who are none the worse for being left to cool their heels for a bit. Only the one door, and one window looking out to the square and the railings of what is called an area in these establishments. Some Hepplewhite chairs and a pretty little oval mahogany table, on which lay today's issues of *The Times* and the *Morning Chronicle* together with sheets of notepaper and an inkstand and quills.

It looked as if the deceased might have been writing something, or about to write something, for several of these sheets had been drawn to the edge of the table before a chair. But there was no sign of any written matter, and with a fleeting thought that the unfortunate fellow might have seen something in the news which had inspired him to despair and his rash act—for I am a man who always thinks of everything—I took up *The Times*; and in so doing fell into a fresh mystery. There was another paper there, of a different kind and quality from that on the table, slipped into the folds of the news-sheet perhaps as if for hasty concealment; it had been creased before, was somewhat finger-marked and bore six lines of the most nonsensical doggerel you ever saw in your life. Here they are exactly as they were set down: We're all in the dumps,/For diamonds is trumps;//The kittens are gone to St Paul's./The babies are bit,//The Moon's in a fit,/And the houses are built without walls.//

A mere instant was enough to take that in, while Major Finchingfield was now bending down to examine the body closer; and welcome to the exercise. He did not see me looking at the paper and I have often pondered since on what a different course this remarkable mystery might have taken had I disclosed my discovery to him there and then—and so may the genteel reader if she so pleases—but it is not my habit to disclose discoveries before I know what they mean myself. Moreover, there were several aspects to this knowing-looking gentleman which I was not all that satis-fied about; I had not much cared for his sly observation that Lady Dorothea might explain more about this Captain Fénelon than he could, and I entertained a shrewd suspicion that he privately considered a Bow Street man to be very small beer. As he straightened up, therefore, I slipped the paper back into the folds of *The Times* again and assumed a somewhat moonish expression, saying humbly, 'Well, Major? I shall be particular obliged for any observations a gentleman of your experience may have.'

He gave that curt nod of his head. 'It looks plain enough.' He was holding the pistol and he laid it down on *The Times* newspaper itself. 'That's French make,' he continued. 'Issue to the Chasseurs; and most likely this poor devil's property. A damned good weapon too at close quarters, though it spits powder grains everywhere. Plain enough,' he repeated. 'Only question is why the fellow did it.'

'No, sir,' I announced. 'There's another. You say you knew the man. So tell me, if you will; would you call him a gentleman?'

'Oh, begod, yes,' the major answered. 'He was a bit cracked over certain matters, mind you; mainly Boney. But uncommon proper otherwise. All these French officers are. They'll do their damnedest to kill you, but all in the politest manner possible and no offence meant.'

'Then will you tell me,' I demanded warmly, 'why he should choose to make this horrid mess in the house of a kindly and generous lady who couldn't ever have done him any harm? Be damned to it, that ain't the act of a gentleman.'

'No more it ain't,' he agreed. But before he could get any further there was a scuffling and squealing and cursing outside the door, and it was flung open to reveal Miss Harriet half dragging Master Maggsy by the ear. 'We'll not have this,' she announced. 'Demned if we will, Sturrock. If you don't dust the arse of this little wretch's pants for him I'll do it meself. Or did you set him on to it?'

'Why, Miss Harriet,' I enquired, all innocence. 'Set him on to what?'

'Sniffing and prying among the servants, for one thing. Threatening the garden boy, as shouldn't have been in the house at all. Getting the scullery wench up against the sink and frightening the wits out of her. Not that she's got any.'

But then she caught sight of the mortality on the floor, and stopped short with Maggsy forgotten. He lost no time about wriggling out of her clutch as slippery as an eel, while the excellent old lady blenched somewhat behind her beak of a nose, but then recovered herself enough to extract a snuff-box from her reticule and take a hearty pinch before observing, 'That's a demned fine mess. No demned consideration at all. We shall have to get contractors in to clean this place. Can't ask the servants to do it. An' what the devil are you standing gazing at him for?' she demanded. 'Ain't you got nothing better to do?'

'Ma'am,' I told her earnestly, 'there's nothing we want to do more than save Lady Dorothea and yourself any further trouble. But there's certain matters here we don't understand.'

'Begod,' she said, 'it looks plain enough to me. An' I've a message for you from Dorothea. She asks will you be good enough to see what has to be done, as she's somewhat otherwise engaged presently.'

'It goes without saying,' I promised, and added to Maggsy, 'You get out of here and send Jagger in to me,' I had one eye on Major Finchingfield lest he should take the pistol off *The Times*, move the news-sheet and discover that other paper underneath, but he was standing in a manner of polite attention, and I went on again to Miss Harriet, 'And I must question Mr Masters.'

'Question Masters?' she repeated. 'You'll be demned clever if you can, for he's been struck speechless with a stroke. Can't get a word out; an' he'll be fortunate if he ever does again. I never see such a pickle in a respectable house,' she cried. 'Masters lying as helpless as a log, Millichip the valet nowhere to be found just when he might make himself useful for once, Georgina sicking her heart out with her maid holding her head, an' that lot in the drawing-room still sitting about like crows. What the devil are you keeping them here for?'

I struck my forehead like a man vexed with his own foolishness. 'Be damned, I'd clean forgot 'em,' I announced, thinking that there would never be a better chance of getting shot of Major Finchingfield. 'So will you do me another kindness, Major?' I asked. 'Will you take all their names and addresses, and then let 'em go? A certain authority, as comes natural to you, but tell 'em it's a mere formality and they're not like to hear any more of it.' It struck me for an instant that he was not all that willing; I had a quick notion that he would have liked to be left alone with the corpse for a bit, but he gave his little nod and I continued, 'I must remain here to see to the arrangements; notify the proper officers, and have this fellow taken to the mortuary. But after that, if you've no more important occasions tonight, I'll beg the honour and pleasure of your company at supper.'

He shot me another of his considering looks before replying, 'Aye. I fancy it'd be as well. I'm bound to stop by the Horse Guards first to see if there's any fresh orders issued; I'm expecting my posting to Brussels to join Lancey any time. But apart from that I'm free enough.'

I put on my somewhat moonish manner once more. 'Then it's settled. I'll pick you up close by the Whitehall entrance at eight o'clock and we'll go to Beale's Chop House by Charing Cross. It's a place much infested by Members of Parliament, but Beale keeps a very fair claret to console us for the nuisance of 'em.'

He still seemed disposed to linger, and went with something of an ill-grace, but once the door was closed behind him I went on, 'We don't want to stay in here any longer than we must, ma'am, but there's some questions I'm bound to ask. First, who introduced that Major Finching-field to Lady Dorothea's salon? And he he ever been here before?'

'Demned if I know,' she answered promptly. 'An' don't much care. But I've never seen him until today.'

'So ho,' I mused. 'Well, maybe it don't matter all that much. Now this unfortunate gentleman. What was his business with Lady Dorothea?'

'Same as several others,' Miss Harriet snapped. 'Another of her lame ducks. An' if you want more than that you must ask Dorothea herself. But I'll not let you fret her any more today, Sturrock. I'll have you put out of the house first. She's beside herself with worry for Masters.'

So I was being baulked, I thought. But I asked, 'How bad is he? I must discover what so frightened him.'

'He's demnation bad,' she retorted. 'And it's plain what frightened him, yer dunderhead. Heard that bang and came to see what it was. The sight of that lot's enough to frighten anybody, and he's an old man and frail. We've been concerned about him for some time past.'

'Very well,' I agreed, though I still doubted it, 'we know what frightened him. So now there's just this one last thing.' I took the sheet of paper with its silly, mysterious verse of doggerel out from under *The Times*. 'Can you hazard a guess what this is, or what it may mean?'

Just for an instant, like those occasions with Major Finchingfield, I was certain that the clever old lady knew more than she was prepared to let on. It is not all that easy to pull the wool over Jeremy Sturrock's eyes, and there was a quick, sudden look of surprise and recognition which even she could not quite conceal. She cried, 'God's sakes, have you gone out of your wits as well? It's an old nursery rhyme, man. Why, I used to sing it myself when I was no more than knee high. But God knows what it means. It don't have a meaning.' She stopped, taking another sideways look at the paper, and then asked, 'Where did you find it?'

I nodded to the copy of *The Times* on the table. 'Folded into that news-sheet. I fancy the deceased must have put it there, in concealment for some reason.'

It was very plain she seemed relieved by that. 'Aye,' she said, 'That's the most likely. It's the kind of crackpot thing he would do. Well, we don't need it lying about,' she added briskly. 'I can't put up with untidiness in the place.' She folded it up small and thrust it into her reticule, then took out the snuff to help herself to another pinch, giving me a half wink and saying, 'Dorothea don't approve of this.'

An uncommon quick-thinking old lady, I thought with some admiration; and it was no great matter. I could remember the verse well enough, and the handwriting; somewhat sloping backwards and done with a broad-cut quill. 'So I'll not keep you any longer in this unwholesome place, ma'am,' I told her.

'And thank God for it,' she retorted. But when I opened the door for her she lingered a minute, and then added, 'See here, Mr Sturrock, it's plain enough that that fool shot himself. Let it be at that and don't get fretting Dorothea with questions. She's got troubles of her own.'

'So ho,' I said again, very soft, as the old lady left; but then turned to a more careful examination of the corpse now that I was at last left alone with him. A distasteful task, and too damned distasteful to search him as well, attired in my best Hanover Square frockcoat and pantaloons, for to be plain I did not consider it all that necessary. But I paid particular attention to powder burns on the right-hand side of his coat collar and to the state of his hands, and I noted also that there was a quill lying on the floor close by his left. 'So there we have it,' I mused. 'And I don't like the look of it.'

Having next received Major Finchingfield's list of the other gentlemen present at the salon, seen him safely out of the house, and dispatched Jagger to notify the Parish Constable and summon the mortuary men to remove the body, I retired to the more salubrious air of the drawing-room to hear what Maggsy had to say for himself. 'You spavined dromedary,' I apostrophised him, 'you goose-witted, monkey-faced, blue-bottomed baboon, how often have I told you that in the whole Art and Science of Detection there's no worse crime than letting yourself get caught?'

'How was I to know that the old besom'd come roaring down into the servants' hall screeching for Miss Georgina's maid?' he retorted. 'Do you want to know what I discovered, or don't you?'

There are two ways with Master Maggsy; either to knock him senseless or to be as patient as you can, and commonly it is best to be patient. It was a sore trial, but I said, 'Mind you manners when speaking of Miss Harriet. Apart from that, what did you discover?'

'Nothing,' he answered and then, seeing my face darkening again, continued hurriedly, 'what I mean is that that's rummy in itself. Like a dog that ought to bark but don't. What you're after is whether that cove corpussed himself or got corpussed, and rising out of that whether anybody left the house in a hurry hard after the bang. Well, there wasn't.'

'No,' I said, pondering on it a minute. 'It don't make sense. That can't be right. Or it's damnation awkward if it is.'

'It's got to be damnation awkward then,' he observed. 'See now, I'm outside the front door in our chaise; and it's certain nobody come out that way. That scullery wench, Amy, was scouring out the copper in the scullery, as overlooks the tradesman's entrance, and she never see anybody neither. And Jagger's in the peach house, which is close by the garden door to the mews, and no more did he.'

'Jagger's in the peach house?' I repeated. 'What the devil was he doing there? And who was standing by my horses?'

'One of the stable-men, as Jagger give a shilling to, to perform the office. Jagger's sweet on Miss Polly Andrews, who is Miss Georgina's maid,' Maggsy explained kindly.

'He reckons to have a ride on her before he's done, even if he has to marry her to get it.'

'Does he indeed?' I asked. 'This grows to be most wonderful romantic. We now have Jagger in the peach house with his Miss Polly Andrews. Pray continue, Master Maggsy.'

'You know how the garden is?' he enquired. 'There's the end wall against the mews and a door in the middle, where they bring the muck in from the stables, and a lean-to peach house on either side of it. Well, then, when they're wore out from their labours in the afternoons the gardener, Mr McKechnie, always sleeps in one of 'em, and the garden boy in t'other. It makes you weep for 'em, don't it? The way they toil and slave for the idle and unheeding rich. So as it happens today Jagger gives this garden boy another penny to keep watch in the servants' hall and run to fetch Miss Polly Andrews if she was called for; but don't you let on to Jagger as I told you or he'll gut me for it. So there it is; I asked Jagger and he says there wasn't nobody went out by that door neither. Of course,' the sweet child added judicially, 'he might not've noticed if he was already astride Miss Polly Andrews, but I don't reckon he'd go galloping her in broad daylight. Leastways, not in the glasshouse. And, anyway, I fancy she's giving him a bit of the old come on but keep off.'

'A pretty recital,' I announced. 'You should have it put to music. And if Jagger's flinging his money about like that I'll dock his wages. But it makes the mystery worse confounded. What about this scullery maid? Can you believe her?'

'Well, she ain't no more than a ha'penny in the shilling,' he said. 'And all she's got on her mind is what Jagger wants to be giving Miss Polly Andrews. But even she can see somebody going past the window.'

'Did you glean anything else?' I asked.

He shook his head. 'Not a lot. Only that the corpuss was admitted to the house by Benson, the footman, a little while before you lot arrived for the tea-party, and he was put in that little side room, where Lady Dorothea stayed talking to him for some time.'

'And nothing more?' I pressed the wretch.

This time he grinned. 'Only about Miss Georgina Wilde-Hookham, who the scullery maid says is a right rare piece. She's got sent up from the country, and Miss Polly Andrews with her, to keep 'em both in order. Seems that she was having a rollick, or about to have a rollick with some young cove at Hookham Priors, but they found it out in time and the young cove's been sent for a soldier. I never heard the whole of it, as that's where the old besom catched me with the scullery maid and the treacherous little tit screeched out that I was pestering her.'

'That's no great importance,' I told him. 'Though it don't surprise me, and if I wasn't more concerned with this other matter I should feel inclined to ask how that young lady comes to know so much about things which ain't her business. But we've no time for that. I don't like the look of what we've got on our plate already, so here's another instruction; and see you bear it well in mind. I'm supping with this Major Finchingfield tonight, and it's very likely that he'll be riding in the chaise with us for a bit. If you happen to be there with us you'll keep your big mouth shut about this affair, for I mean to let him think I'm satisfied it's a simple case of suicide.'

'What ho,' the little monster enquired. 'So you're meaning to fox him as well, are you?'

'All I'm meaning,' I said, 'is that it's far from simple.'

Two

There was such a coming and going about the Horse Guards that we were obliged to stand our horses well down White-hall, and then had sharp words with one of the sentries, who had the damned impudence to tell me that he'd never heard of Major Finchingfield. The traffic in London grows thicker year by year, and it will not be long now before the place chokes itself up altogether. But on this occasion I was thankful to see the bustle, for seemingly the latest intelligence was worse again with the afternoon telegraphs sending fresh reports of the Frenchies' further advance to the Belgian frontier. Government clerks scurrying as they'd never scurried in their lives before, mounted messengers galloping in and out, carriages racing up thick with the dust of long journeys, officers leaping from 'em, and the common crowd of idlers that are always with us raising a cheer now and again.

For my part I hoped to God that in another week or so they might still have something to cheer about, but Maggsy was all agog with the excitement of it. 'D'you reckon they'll have Boney's head off when they catches him this time?' he asked. 'God's whiskers, I'd admire to see that. And I'd admire to see this set-to when it starts.'

'They've got to catch Boney first,' I observed shortly.
'And you may thank God in advance that you're not like to
see the battle,' I added, little knowing how much more than
slightly mistaken I was. But it is a merciful Providence that
we are not given to see the future; and, to tell the truth, I was
more concerned presently with the perplexities of Lady
Dorothea and Jagger's deceitfulness—the rascal sitting
there looking as pleased with himself as a cock robin and as
innocent as a pint of milk.

Fortunately, Major Finchingfield appeared at a brisk
pace before much more could be said, being pleased to speak
favourably of my cattle and smart little turnout in general,
and we picked our way out of the clattering throng for the
few minutes' trot to Beale's. Here Maggsy and Jagger were
banished to their own devices—very likely to plot fresh
villainy—but ordered to bring the chaise back at an
appointed time, and we addressed ourselves to an Aylesbury
duck, a nice cut of rare done sirloin, a particular fine ripe
Stilton, and a pint or two of claret. Moreover, the Major
entertained me most excellently with his reminiscences of
Wellington in India and the Spanish campaigns, and his
views on the present situation.

'There's certain quarters pressing the duke for a general
attack into France,' he said, 'but it ain't practical. It'd mean
an advance on a long front with the line stretched too thin;
and much of it's too raw. Not even Lancey could shift that
lot in time, and he can move an army quicker than any man
in the world.' He plainly had a large admiration for this
officer and added, 'Never been a quartermaster-general to
match him before, and the remarkable thing is that he's an
American. Born in New York of an old Huguenot family,
and was with Wellington in Spain. The duke demanded a

knighthood for him for his services there.'

It crossed my mind briefly that the good major was going into deep detail to establish his own knowledge and position; but it is never my habit to check a man when he feels like talking, as you always discover more that way, and he continued, 'He's only just married. Wellington broke his honeymoon, for he'd not been wedded a week before the Duke sent for him to post out to Brussels. Lady de Lancey's a Scots girl, Magdalene Hall as was, and they're both deep in love.* She's now gone away to Brussels herself. And that,' the major finished with the air of answering a question before it is asked, 'is how I came to be present at Lady Dorothea's tea-party this afternoon. For Magdalene de Lancey's a friend of the family; and seeing I was in London she begged to call and present her affections, and inform her ladyship of their address in the rue Royale.'

'And very proper,' I observed. 'Do you know the other young military gentlemen who was present? A Captain ffoulkes?'

'Can't say I do.' The major laughed, well into his third pint of claret, 'You may recollect I called him a teacup soldier, but don't mistake me, Mr Sturrock; I've seen that sort before. If the common foot soldiers hold, poor devils, Boney might well be halted before 'em. But if he's to be routed and beat for good and all it'll be young fellows like ffoulkes who'll do it.'

'No doubt assisted by young ladies like Miss Georgina Wilde-Hookham,' I mused. 'Who would appear to have

---

*This was one of the many tragedies of Waterloo. Colonel Sir William de Lancey was struck by a cannon ball while riding beside Wellington during the closing stages of the battle. His young wife afterwards rode out from Brussels to search for him, and he died in her arms six days later.

either second sight or military genius. Tell me, Major Finchingfield, have you ever heard of this place Waterloo before?'

The major glanced at me shrewdly. 'Looking for spies, are you?' He shook his head. 'That cock won't fight. To be sure I've heard talk of Waterloo. See now, Mr Sturrock, there's always talk and letter-writing in an idle army. Your pert little miss was repeating something she's picked up. And I wouldn't say it was from Captain ffoulkes either.' He paused to relight his pipe, and then added, 'I can tell you that the late Captain Fénelon had a considerable knowledge of military matters.'

So ho, I thought; so we've got around to it in the end. 'You're saying that the young lady had some connection with the deceased?' I asked.

He gave me another shrewd look. 'I'm saying that if you want to know more about Fénelon you might do worse than ask Miss Georgina.'

'To be sure,' I agreed. 'I might. But there's no need. I'm satisfied now that the man shot himself.' I related the total of our investigations at some length, though omitting certain matters, and finished, 'You observed yourself that there was little time for a murderer to escape. And I'll add to that he'd have had to be invisible as well, for it's certain that nobody was seen to pass out of that house within a few minutes after the shot.'

'You see what that leaves you with, don't you?' he enquired. 'Might I ask, Mr Sturrock, did you think to search the body?'

'No, sir, I did not,' I replied. 'I did not see the need, and such tasks are not part of my position. It will be searched at the mortuary. And you may be sure that if anything suspicious is found I shall be informed of the fact.'

'Aye,' the major asked, 'but when? And how will they know what's suspicious?'

I was beginning to dislike the turn this conversation was taking. 'Tomorrow,' I told him sharply. 'And I shall be called to the inquest. Where the whole matter will be very fully debated.'

'By tomorrow I might have my marching orders,' he murmured. 'And I've a particular interest in this affair now. But I see your boy there at the door looking about for us,' he added. 'Would he perhaps be bringing a message?'

'Only to advise us that our horses are waiting,' I replied, shorter still.

Not in the best of tempers I called for the server to settle the reckoning, for no man likes to have it hinted that he has been remiss in his duties, but our inquisitive major was by no means done yet. 'Then that's fine and convenient,' he announced. 'I propose we go to this mortuary ourselves, Mr Sturrock.'

'What, sir?' I cried, now finally dumbfounded. 'At this hour?'

'It'll do as well as any other,' he observed mildly, drawing out a heavy silver watch to consult it. 'Not much after ten. Mr Sturrock,' he continued. 'I'll tell you something you may not know. The Office of the Quartermaster-General is sometimes concerned with many other matters besides supplies and moving armies to the commander's strategy. Sir William de Lancey demands a well-informed intelligence; and I'm asking your assistance. So shall we go to this mortuary? And go fast?'

The night had turned dark, heavy and sultry, and it was a

silent drive, for the major seemed to be communing with his
own thoughts and there was little I could trust myself to say.
Even Maggsy was unwontedly silent after asking 'Are we
going resurrectioning now, then?' and getting himself
sharply admonished for it; while Jagger was doubtless
dreaming of his Miss Polly Andrews.

Not unnaturally, these mortal repositories are always set
in the most dismal and secluded parts of the parish, and this
at St Mary-le-bone was no exception. A close alley, a single
dim bracket lantern throwing an uncertain light on the
scene, and already a whiff of death and corruption in the air
enough to make our horses restless. On one side the high
wall bounding a paupers' graveyard, and on the other the
black brick of a low, gloomy and inhospitable edifice with
small and heavily barred windows; both wall and bars being
entirely unneccessary precautions, since those that are
inside cannot get out, while few of those outside have any
desire to go in.

But without wasting any further time on such profound
philosophical reflections I got down from the chaise and
rapped smartly on the door of the keeper's lodge with the
head of my cane. This place, too, was strangely dark, and
there was no answer. The only sounds were the nervous
jingle of our harness, the chaise creaking as the major himself
descended, and Jagger muttering to his horses to quieten
them. Nor did a more peremptory rattle bring any response
or sign of light appearing at the windows, but now Master
Maggsy chose to observe loudly, 'Maybe the keeper reckons
it's one of his customers got up to ask after his health. In his
situation I shouldn't fancy coming out to no knocking in the
middle of the night neither.'

'The rascal's probably dead drunk,' I told the major.

'But, by God, I'll have him out,' I said, beating an impatient tattoo which raised the echoes; and hard upon it, breaking the next uneasy silence, Maggsy screeched, 'There's a door open here.'

He was a few paces off, close by the double gates by which the unfortunates are admitted to this lodging, and in the dim glow of our carriage lamps he seemed to vanish suddenly into a pit of blackness. 'I don't fancy this lot,' he muttered. 'There's something moving,' he cried; and this was followed by a strange unearthly moan, a shriek of terror and then such a pandemonium of yells, curses and howls as you might have thought all the devils in hell were out. The horses shied and damned near bolted, adding their clatter and Jagger's observations to the uproar as he tried to hold 'em, the major rapped out a most remarkable military oath, and I added several more of my own while Maggsy screeched, 'God's cripes, they've got me. It's the corpusses broke loose. Lie still, you bastards,' he screamed as I plunged through the gates into the darkness to him.

There was nothing to be seen, but from the scuffling and panting he seemed to be trying to kick himself free or to be struggling with something close by, and as I groped out blindly for the little wretch there was another whispering moan and a cold hand seemed to reach up from below to clutch at my knees. I uttered a startled curse myself, stumbling over the wet cobbles, but it is a sturdy corpse which can outdo me when my temper gets roused and, roaring for somebody to bring a light, I laid about right and left with my cane, feeling it strike something solid and fetching fresh screeches from Maggsy. 'God's whiskers,' he shrieked, 'go easy, will you? You damn near had my eye out then. It ain't me you want, it's him. There's a corpus on the floor there, crawling about.'

It was a scene of some slight confusion when the major brought a lamp from the chaise a second later, for I was clutching Maggsy by the hair while we were both straddled over a further body lying between our feet. The little fool let off a fresh shriek at the sight of the pallid face staring up at us, its mouth opening and shutting like a codfish, but by the strong reek of gin now perceptible I recognised at once who it was. 'Wilkes,' I announced. 'Be damned to him. The mortuary keeper.'

'Stand back,' says the major, approaching closer with the lamp and then asking. 'Now, my man; what's happened here?'

'God rot 'em,' the fellow got out, as near as you could make it. 'Body-snatching.'

'Which one?' the major demanded urgently. 'Which body? Speak up, now.'

But the only answer he got this time was a horrid, rasping snore dying away in a catch of breath, and I cried, 'The rascal's dead drunk.'

'He was drunk, maybe,' Major Finchingfield said, 'but he's dead enough now. He's a damned sight too dead. See here.' He rolled the head over none to gently. 'He was struck down by something a good bit heavier than that little cane of yours, Mr Sturrock.'

'It wasn't me,' Maggsy started shrilly. 'He was crawling about. He catched at me . . .'

'His last effort,' the major interrupted. 'Be quiet; and get out.'

I have never seen the little monster move so fast as the major straightened up to flash the lamp about; and a sweet sight it was, what with the damp cobbles, the slate slabs for the cadavers, each with its trickle of water to keep 'em cool in this sultry weather, shadows over the whole, and Wilkes lying there in the pool of light. He had never been a pretty object in his life, but he was a damned sight worse now, seeming to be staring covetously at a small, glinting object lodged in a crack of the stones. It was a golden sovereign, and I said, 'It's plain to see what happened. The rascal was always half soaked in gin, and somebody comes to the lodge, offers him a sovereign to let 'em in here, and then puts him down so he shan't tell no tales. But who, and what the devil for?'

The major's lips drew back in what looked like an uncommonly unkind grin in the lamplight. 'I'd say the second part of that's plain enough as well. But we'd best take a look to make sure.'

It was by no means the most salubrious of occupations in that horrid vault. There were half a dozen slabs, three of them occupied by anonymous bundles of rough, damp canvas, and it was no more than the work of a second to lift the sheet off each to survey what lay beneath. A second was more than enough to gaze on the greenish, lifeless face wavering in the candlelight, and enough to make sure that whatever these unfortunates might have claimed to be in life not one of them had been Captain Louis Fénelon, one time of Bonaparte's Twelfth Chasseurs.

It was well past midnight before we had finished the necessities there: notified the parish authorities once more, had sharp words with a frightened fool of a watchman who came peering round the corner with his lantern like a clown in a pantomime, dispatched him to fetch a surgeon—a saucy young rascal not above twenty, and half tipsy—and finally put the mortuary keeper to bed in his own lodging-house. To satisfy the major I set Maggsy and Jagger knocking up the cottages adjacent, but, as I expected, they got nothing but dusty answers; one surly rogue driving Maggsy off with a broomstick and an idiot woman shrieking that there was a riot in the dead house. Likewise for the appearance of it, I had all the lamps lit and searched the mortuary and the keeper's lodge, but expected nothing and got nothing. In short, if Captain Fénelon had had any belongings about him they had all vanished into such thin air, even the pistol, as Captain Fénelon himself.

With that clear there was nothing more we could do and I gave the order to move off, offering politely to set the major down at his lodging if he would give Jagger the directions. This however he seemed unwilling to do, saying only, 'Any way back you're going will suit me,' though he climbed in the chaise with alacrity; and then when we were rattling along at a brisk pace, with Jagger and the horses smelling their stable and glad of it, he enquired. 'Will there be an inquest on Fénelon now?'

'I'm damned if I know,' I confessed. 'I've never before had a case like this. Whether you can have an inquest without a body is an uncommon nice point. There'll be an inquiry; as there'll be an inquest on the man Wilkes, and no doubt a verdict of murder. I shall be called to both; and so will you, I fancy.'

He whistled softly between his teeth. 'What if I've had my posting orders by then?'

'Likewise again, I don't know,' I admitted. 'In the present emergency it might be allowed that military duties are overriding.'

'Very likely.' He seemed somewhat abstracted, 'But what of yourself? Will you set up a search for Fénelon?'

'You might as well search for a pin in a haystack,' I told him.

'Best search for a kerridge first,' Maggsy must needs chime in. 'There must have been at least two coves about this job and they couldn't have dared carry the corpuss off in their arms. Even in Mary-le-bone somebody'd be sure to cry out "What ho, mates, what's that you got there?" Nor they couldn't have had a common hackney, as it makes your blood run cold to think of what a hackney driver would reply if they says "Drive us to the mortewry, my man, as we wish to snitch a corpuss". And a phaeton or a chaise wouldn't be big enough to do it easy. We done a resurrection once, by Medmenham,' he informed the astonished major. 'That was in a chaise like this, and we had to lay the corpuss down on the footboard with his head hanging out one side and his feet t'other. Lucky it was in the country, and pitch dark and pissing with rain or we should've been spotted for certain. So they must've had a closed town kerridge,' he concluded. 'Like Lady Dorothea's' he added as an afterthought. 'Come to think of it, that town and country coach at Hanover Square'd just about fit the bill.'

He paused for breath, and I cried, 'Be quiet, you little monster,' but the major was unseasonably amused. 'Come now, Mr Sturrock,' he protested, 'the boy's got his wits about him. And they seem to be in pretty fair working order.'

'His wits are as unruly as his tongue,' I retorted, 'and I'll not have such talk. There are hundreds of town and country coaches in London.' The major seemed to look at me somewhat strangely, and I said, 'I doubt the need of much investigation. Captain Fénelon was plainly a common suicide, and the drunken rascal Wilkes is of no great account

to anybody. But if there is to be an inquiry it must start with
Fénelon. His mode and manner of life and his associates.
And as to that, you'll be one of the first persons we shall ask.'

The major laughed to himself, but answered, 'And I'll tell
you willingly. What little I know about the poor devil, and
that's most of what he's told me himself. He's been much
about the Horse Guards for some time past, begging for
employment.'

'A Frenchman begging for employment?' I enquired.
'What sort?'

'Against Boney,' Major Finchingfield replied simply.
'But not against France. It ain't impossible. There's nobody
so bitter as the man who sets up a hero for himself and then
comes to discover that his hero ain't so heroic after all. I told
you he was in the retreat from Moscow.'

At this hour of the night, with the air growing ever more
sultry and thunderous, Jagger was making a spanking pace
towards Tottenham Court, but seemingly the major was in
no hurry. 'By God, that campaign was bungled from the
start,' he continued. 'Before the Grand Army reached
Smolensk on the way out they'd lost near a third of their
effective strength, and their horses were dying by the hundred. And if the advance was bad the retreat was worse.
They were more than half starving when old Kutuzov cut
'em up at the Berezina crossing.'

'*The Times* newspaper carried a very full account of the
defeat,' I pointed out.

'No doubt,' he agreed imperturbably. 'So you'll know
that Boney left his army to fend for itself at a place called
Smorgon, and bolted for Paris. And Fénelon reckoned that if
the Emperor could desert, so could he. He set out for East
Prussia, stayed there for a few months, and then got himself

here expecting to be welcomed with open arms. What he got was a spell in the Rochester hulks, and then Dartmoor Prison.'

'We are now approaching Oxford Street, Major Finchingfield,' I reminded him. 'Only another minute or so from my chambers. But very little further on with Captain Fénelon.'

'Very little further you can get with him,' the major answered. 'He was released when Boney abdicated last year, but he hadn't been treated any too gently by his fellow officer prisoners, and he elected to remain in this country.'

'So he's been living here at liberty for a year or more. By what means?' I asked. 'And what employment was he seeking?'

'The means I don't know, though I could hazard a guess.' As I could myself, I thought; and more than a guess, for Miss Harriet had as good as told me so. But I did not mention the matter, and the major added, 'As for the employment, and to put it simple, he was offering himself as a spy. He was always certain sure that Boney would break out again.'

'So ho,' I murmured. 'And was he taken up on the offer?'

'He was not. Nobody quite trusts a deserter, Mr Sturrock, not even from the other side. And he was reckoned to be getting a bit of a pest, with a bee in his bonnet. For my part I was sorry for the man; and I was interested in his accounts of the Russian Campaign.'

'And what were his views of the present impending battle?' I enquired.

The major laughed. 'Very plain. He had no doubt that Boney will break through, and we shall either have to make peace on our knees or have it all to do again.'

'Enough to drive any man to despair,' I commented as Jagger swung us round into Soho Square and pulled up before my door. 'Much less in his position. So there you have it, Major. Disappointed and unwanted, having lived a life as near as possible to hell for the last three years, and fearful of the future. Quite enough for suicide. It's my opinion that he saw something in the newspapers this afternoon which drove him suddenly and finally to the rash act. There you have the answers to all our questions.'

'Except why his body was snatched,' the major replied. 'None the less I hope you may be right, Mr Sturrock. For if you ain't there could be another explanation, and one not quite so convenient. I'll leave you to reckon it over. But, for now, where may I find you for the next day or two; that is if I don't get my orders.'

It was plain that our businesslike major did not mean to be shouldered out of the affair if he could help it, but reflecting that he could find me anyhow if he set his mind to it I said, 'The Bow Street office will always know where I am; and if I'm at liberty I step into the Brown Bear in Drury Lane most evenings.' Then reflecting that there was no harm in keeping an eye on the major as well, in particular discovering where he was lodging, as well as putting Jagger in the way of earning half a guinea for himself, I added, 'But don't get down now, Major. By the look of the sky it'll be tippling with rain any minute, and I dare say my man will take you on where you want to go if we ask him kindly, for he's a good fellow.'

It crossed my mind that he was not too eager for the kindness, but then a grumble of thunder coming close seemed to echo my words and he admitted himself obliged. So, with a final nod to Jagger that he was to come up and report to me on his return, we parted politely with mutual expressions of esteem.

It was now close on one o'clock and more than time for a last nightcap, a pipe or two and a space for quiet reflection: and there is no task which Maggsy performs with greater willingness than setting out our tobacco jar and the Madeira. When that was done however, he announced, 'It's a rum go, this lot. Was you gammoning him, or was he gammoning you?'

'A bit of each,' I replied. 'But I fancy the honours lie with me for the present.'

'I hope they do,' he observed darkly. 'If you ask me, that cove's uncommon fly. And what about that corpuss? Did he do it himself, or was it done for him?'

'There's little doubt that it was done for him. First, he was writing something, for there was a quill lying close by his left hand and a small stain of ink on the forefinger of that hand; and whatever he had been writing was removed. Second, there was no sign of powder-marking on either hand, although Major Finchingfield himself informed me that the pistol used is a good weapon but spits powder everywhere. Third, there was powder-burning on the right side of his coat collar and to a lesser extent on the right shoulder. A man intending suicide might well be somewhat agitated,' I finished, 'but he can't be so absent-minded as to shoot himself from the right when he's left-handed. In short, there was another person present. And Major Finchingfield suspects or is aware of that fact.'

Maggsy shook his head. 'There wasn't nobody come out of that house hard after the shot. That's certain. I don't like this turn-up. If you ask me, we'd best let it alone. Unless you want to find your Lady Dorothea up to her snout in it.'

'We can't let it alone,' I told him. 'Not with our Major Finchingfield so interested in the matter. And don't let your fanciful poetics carry you too far.'

'It wasn't fanciful poetics carried that corpuss off,' the obstinate wretch retorted. 'It was a private town kerridge. And what was that done for, anyway?'

'Either to make sure that the certain evidence of murder should not be discovered; or to find something which Captain Fénelon might have had about his person. And as to that, bring me the inkstand and paper.' Somewhat mystified, he brought me these implements and I occupied myself for a minute or so writing out the doggerel I had found, complete with the strokes and double strokes, while explaining how I had come across it. 'I don't say for sure that this is what they were looking for,' I added, 'but it could well have been.'

Maggsy studied it critically. 'It's just dead daft, ain't it?' he asked. 'But could be what he was writing?'

'No,' I said. 'The original paper, which Miss Harriet most noticeably took away from me to keep for herself, had been folded and refolded several times; and the writing was on it before the folds. Moreover, it didn't strike me as being Fénelon's hand.'

'So Miss Harriet's in it as well, is she?' Maggsy asked. 'Well, I wouldn't mind seeing that old besom catched for something. I don't like her a lot, anyway.'

'Don't let your fancies run away with you,' I warned him again. 'But we also have this.' I took out the list of names which Major Finchingfield had obligingly set down for me, half a dozen or so of 'em, and not of much import except I noted that Captain ffoulkes was lodging not much more

than a stone's throw away from Hanover Square, in Portland Place. But there was one of somewhat greater interest
in the light of various conversations. ' "The Reverend
Doctor Erasmus Slocombe, M.A., Ph.D., of Nine, Sadler's
Walk, Sadler's Wells",' I read out. 'Now he's another of the
family dependants,' I continued, 'and he's frequently at
Lady Dorothea's salon. He was at one time tutor to the late
Lieutenant Lord Hookham, Lady Dorothea's elder brother,
who died in action against the French off the West Indies
some few years ago.'

'I see him,' Maggsy announced. 'Ancient old cove and a
rusty old frockcoat. He come to the house a bit after you
went in, and I noticed him particular as there was a saucy-
looking nursemaid with a most uncommon pair of bouncers
come tittuping by, and he give her the leeriest look I ever see
in my life. I fancy he made a grab at her backside as well the
way she bucked, and I recollect thinking that he should be
ashamed at his age.'

'We're not concerned with his manners and morals,' I said.
'What's more to the point is that when Lady Dorothea
greeted him she asked, "How is your work on the Russian
Campaign progressing, Erasmus?" You don't have to look
far to connect that with Captain Louis Fénelon, late of the
Twelfth Chasseurs.'

'So he's another one?' the horrid child asked. 'God's
tripes, it gets to look as if they're all up to their snouts in it.'

On this observation Jagger returned to the accompaniment of further grumbles of thunder, sundry flashes and a
lash of rain against the windows. The good cheerful fellow
came in announcing, 'Just got the hosses to stable in time, as
there's a rare old storm brewing up. Made a brisk run there
and back, and all cordial on both sides. Took the gentleman

to the King's Arms, by Holborn.'

'The coaching house for Rochester and Harwich,' I mused, 'and that's what you'd expect as he might have to post at any time. Did he treat you right?' I enquired. 'And was you as attentive as befits his rank?'

'Treated me handsome,' Jagger answered with a well-satisfied grin, 'and I'm obliged to you for putting me in the way of it. And I was attentive enough to wait and watch him go in by the front entrance as if he owned the place.'

'Then you've done very well,' I said. 'It ain't by any means all I want to know about the gallant major, but it'll do for a start. So sit down and help yourself.' This is our habit at the end of the day and I waited until he had filled a glass and his own pipe, which Master Maggsy was not slow to imitate, and then observed jovially, 'I dare say you'll be thankful to pick up an extra half-guinea now and again if all I hear about you is true. Setting your cap at a particular young lady in Lady Dorothea's establishment are you, you young rogue?'

The cunning rascal flushed as dark as a beetroot, casting a wicked wrathful look at Maggsy, and I cried. 'Whoa there, now,' before the fists started to fly. 'You needn't set about Maggsy. It wasn't him that told me. I had it from a better quarter when I was questioning the household today. And don't look so put out. There's no harm in it; not unless you've been dipping in where you shouldn't already.'

'She don't give me the chance,' he admitted regretfully.

'Then you be careful,' I warned him, while Maggsy grunted, with his snout in his Madeira, as innocent as a kitten. 'I like to think I stand in the manner of a father to you, my lad,' I said, 'and I wouldn't like to see you bite off more than you can chew. A maid very often picks up tricks from her mistress, and, by what I've heard, Miss Georgina Wilde-Hookham's a right rare handful. Wasn't there some sort of naughtiness at Hookham Priors? The reason why they packed her off up to Town.'

Jagger grinned again. 'Polly swore me to keep secret on that, but I dunno that there's any harm in telling you. So long as he keeps his trap shut,' he added, with another glower at Maggsy. 'Seems they catched Miss Georgina in a clinch with a young fellow close by. According to Polly, there wasn't no harm done yet but it's certain there would have been before long. Son of the parson at the Priors but a regular rip-roaring young devil for all that, so Polly says. So they got him a commission as ensign and packed him off where he'll have other things to think about, then sent Miss Georgina here to Lady Dorothea to take her mind off him. A rascal as wild as Miss Georgina herself, by name of Tom Debenham.'

'And has it taken her mind off him?' I mused. 'And would he, I wonder, be a friend or acquaintance of a certain Captain ffoulkes?'

My good Jagger looked doubtful. 'I dunno about that. Polly's never spoke of that one.'

'Then you shall ask her,' I promised. 'And at the same time pick up any other views from the servants' hall about today's affair. I mean to pay my respects at Hanover Square in the morning after I've reported to the office, and I've no doubt you can contrive to snatch a minute or two with your lady love. After that we shall take a ride out into the country, to Sadler's Wells. But for now we'll take ourselves to our beds, for I've a notion we've a busy day ahead of us.'

Three

The arrangements at the office were a simple matter, with our present Chief Magistrate content to leave most of the police side to me and our Clerk of the Court, old Abel Makepenny. Between us we pretty well run the place, and when I had finished telling him the full tale, Abel was the first to see eye to eye with me that we should do well to walk on eggs in this affair. In respect of Captain Fénelon we agreed that all the indications could just as well point to suicide as anything else, with the vexatious snatching of the body equally as well attributed to the Resurrection Men; while in the case of the man Wilkes there was little evidence one way or the other, since the rascal was reeking of gin and the cobblestones in the mortuary were damnation slippery.

'In short, Abel,' I said, 'I want few questions asked until we know better what the answers are, so that must be my line at the inquest. And we don't want this Major Finching-field called either; not if we can help it. He's got a suspicious nature. I fancy that a plea of military duties should be enough for old Busby, the coroner at Mary-le-bone, but I don't see why his name need be mentioned at all unless he pushes it in himself. And as to that, if he comes here today asking after me, tell him that the date of the inquest ain't been set yet.'

Abel took my points like the shrewd old gentleman he is, and I continued. 'But I want Captain Fénelon investigated. Set young Burchall on to that, and send him about the coffee-houses; in particular, the Grecian in Deveraux Court. That's where the émigrés used to congregate.' But then considering the major again I was struck with an afterthought, and added, 'If Finchingfield don't come here today, Burchall can go to the King's Arms at Holborn and ask there privately if the gentleman's posted yet. We may know where we are with him then. Burchall is to report to me at the Brown Bear at seven tonight.'

Thus having disposed our strategy with enough room to manoeuvre, I left Abel to handle the matter in his own clever way, emerged to find Jagger and Maggsy waiting for me with the chaise, and set a court for our next inquiries; and fresh perplexities.

I was shown into the morning room at Hanover Square and not kept waiting above ten or fifteen minutes, which was well enough, for it gave Jagger time for the instructions I had given him and me leisure to survey the garden from here; a terrace outside the french window, a flight of steps, a plot of grass with rose-beds, etc., the peach houses and the door to the mews. And seemingly Jagger was about his business, for I also observed a young woman appear, hastening along a side-path but after that I turned away from the window as Lady Dorothea entered the room.

She was plainly not overpleased to see me, though asking my pardon for keeping me waiting, but I interposed, 'No, ma'am, I should ask yours for intruding. But I felt bound to wait on you to offer my condolences on that vexatious occurrence yesterday, and to enquire after Mr Masters.'

'Pray never speak of that matter again, Mr Sturrock,' she cried. 'We cannot think what possessed the unhappy gentleman; and grieved as we may be for him it was an act of . . .' She broke off short there and added, 'Masters, I fear, is most seriously unwell.'

'It was an act of gross discourtesy,' I finished for her. 'And would it be ingratitude as well?' I asked. She gave me a sharp look on that, but did not answer otherwise, and I continued, 'I assure you, ma'am, I shall do all I may to save you further inconvenience, but there are certain matters which are not yet quite clear. In short, would it be possible to have a word or two with Mr Masters?'

'It most certainly would not,' she replied, sharper than ever. 'Mr Sturrock, you do not seem to understand, Masters is stricken speechless. He has not spoken a word since yesterday afternoon.'

'Damnation take it,' I observed involuntarily, then just as quick begged her pardon for the lapse. But I begged, 'Ma'am, are you sure of that? Never a word? Not a hint of what it was he saw?'

'I have told you Masters cannot speak,' she answered somewhat coldly. 'Is not that enough? And is it not all too clear what the poor old man saw? What is this mystery, Mr Sturrock? Are you not satisfied?'

It was all too clear that she was getting a touch of the high and mighties, and I said, 'I am, ma'am, I assure you. But there may be other people who ain't. I had a long conversation with Major Finchingfield last night.'

'Major Finchingfield?' she repeated, somewhat at a loss as if she did not recollect the man.

'The other military gentleman besides Captain ffoulkes

present at your salon yesterday. Attached to the staff of Sir
William de Lancey, Quartermaster-General.' With a fresh
suspicion growing on me from the look on her face I went on,
'I was much interested to hear of Sir William's recent
marriage to your friend Miss Magdalene Hall as was; now
Lady de Lancey. Major Finchingfield was telling me that he
called upon you at her express wish, to acquaint you with
their address in Brussels.'

If I had set the lady that rhyming conundrum I had found
yesterday I could not have puzzled her more; nor for that
matter more startled myself. She said. 'Now you have me
quite at a loss, Mr Sturrock. I know of Sir William de
Lancey, of course, having read of him in the newspapers.
But I certainly do not know his wife, nor can I pretend to
claim her as a friend. And complimented as I may be,
neither can I imagine why either of them should wish to
inform me of their address.'

It fetched me up all standing and damned near in a jibe.
Yet at the back of my mind I was not all that surprised. 'So
ho,' I murmured softly, and then enquired. 'Tell me,
ma'am, had you ever met the major before? And if not, who
brought him to your salon yesterday?'

The high and mighties was now very evident. 'I had not,'
she answered. 'And I begin to find your questions a little
impertinent. But if it is of any importance he was introduced
by Captain ffoulkes.'

'It could be of extreme importance,' I told her earnestly.
'Ma'am, I beg you to understand that all I'm asking is with
intent to save you from further inconvenience. Could you
say whether Captain ffoulkes seemed to know the major
well. As it were a military colleague; perhaps in Spain?'

'Captain ffoulkes did not serve in Spain,' she replied. 'For what little it may be worth I fancied he was somewhat puzzled in presenting Major Finchingfield. But more than that I cannot recollect, Mr Sturrock. Need I remind you that there have been certain distractions since then?'

'Distractions enough,' I agreed. It was on the tip of my tongue to tell her that she better had recollect, and recollect quick, but I thought wiser of it and said instead, 'There's still one more question I must ask, ma'am. How long ago was Captain Fénelon presented, and who brought him to you?'

For a minute it was touch and go whether I was turned out of the house there and then. She observed coldly. 'I cannot see any purpose in this catechism. But if you must know, he was brought to me by Doctor Erasmus Slocombe; whom you yourself have met on several occasions. And Doctor Slocombe, at least, is a most respectable old gentleman.'

'And you might change your mind about that too,' I thought to myself, 'if you heard what Master Maggsy had to say about the old goat's antics with a nursemaid yesterday'. But once again I kept a prudent silence though now somewhat at a loss how to prolong the conversation, for Lady Dorothea was plainly itching to be shot of me, while I was just as anxious to stay here long enough for Jagger to discover all he could.

But it was not to be; and the cause of the disaster was that ugly whelp Maggsy again. As I was casting around in my mind for fresh topics to entertain her, even toying with the thought of telling her about the curious removal of Fénelon's corpse from the mortuary last night, she turned somewhat impatiently to glance out of the window; and on the instant she demanded, 'What is this, Mr Sturrock? What is your boy doing?'

In my consternation I spoke somewhat too freely for a lady's company, uttering an uncommonly descriptive curse as I turned myself to view the spectacle. I had expressly ordered the wicked wretch to remain by the chaise and leave the questioning to Jagger, but now there he was as large as life just inside the mews door and clutching a skinny little girl very near as ugly as himself by the hair, she telling him a pretty selection of home truths by the look of it, while another boy just as horrid was doubling up with his hands clasped about himself either from laughter or a punch in the belly; I could not tell which, and did not care. Moreover, Jagger was plainly visible in the peach house door as his Pretty Polly, clutching her skirts, was cantering up the side-path towards the house.

'Pranks and horseplay, ma'am,' I got out, even me flustered. 'Merely boyish pranks,' I cried, at the same time flinging open the window and bawling, 'Maggsy, you blue-arsed camel . . .'

The scene changed as in a pantomime. Maggsy vanishing like a jack-in-the-box through the mews door, with Jagger after him; the boy seizing a wheelbarrow and trundling it off at a trot; the little girl gazing up at the window, letting out a screech as she perceived Lady Dorothea standing here, and then bolting like a hare. In an instant the garden was calm, peaceful and empty again; but the mischief was done.

And mischief it was. My lady addressed me in tones which might have chilled an icicle. 'Mr Sturrock,' says she, 'I fear you presume a little too much. I have heard from Miss Harriet that yesterday you set your boy on to pestering the servants. Please understand that I will not have my staff troubled in this way. And please understand also that when

I require your further assistance or advice I will send for you.'

'Then you'd best send quick,' I retorted, growing hotter as she got colder. 'You might have need of both before long. Do you know what happened last night?' I demanded. 'I'd not meant to affront you with such matters, but now you leave me no choice.'

'Mr Sturrock,' she interrupted with that beautiful courtesy which is the hallmark of our true British nobility, 'I have several pressing duties to attend to. May I request you to withdraw.'

So I was dismissed with a flea in my ear, not even the grace of a footman to show me out, baulked, baffled, and threatening to break every bone in Maggsy's wicked body to the square, starting with the neck. Jagger had lost no time getting back, waiting there with a look which said the affair was no fault of his, though Maggsy was keeping his distance, hands in pockets, whistling to himself, and eyes turned up to heaven with the innocence of an angel. Not wishing to create an ungenteel scene in Hanover Square, I could not trust myself to speak, but bundled him into the chaise like a sack of mouldy oats and then said with a voice of strangulation. 'Sadler's Wells, Jagger. And go by the way of the nearest canal, where we may drown the witless jackass.'

Maggsy answered nothing, looking at me out of the corners of his eyes like a mongrel that means to get the first bite, and when we were well out of the square into Oxford Street I made several observations with which I shall not sully these genteel pages. But when I paused to draw breath Maggsy asked sullenly, 'How the hell was I to know you and her would get peering out? If you don't want to hear about the kerridge that carried that corpuss off it's all the same with me.'

'What?' I said, 'What carriage?'

'Plain enough, ain't it?' Maggsy demanded. 'The Hanover Square town and country. I reckoned so all along. See now, what time did it start raining last night? Just gone one o'clock, wasn't it? Well, then, when Jagger goes off to confabulate with Miss Polly Andrews, like you told him, I fancy I'll have a nosey on my own, round the back of the mews where I knows one of the stable-lads named Jebb. And, sure enough, there I find him scrubbing and polishing at the kerridge, and cussing himself into a pox over the state it's in. "God's pickles, Jebby," says I, "that's a right proper mess, where did they get it like that?" and he says, "Damned if I know, as nobody never tells me nothing, but must have been halfway through the bleedin' river and back by the look of it", so whereupon I then take a sniff inside to see if there was any blood and guts, as there ought to be if they'd been carting a corpuss about; but no sign of that, only a bit of stiffish paper trod into the wet on the floor. Which I snitched.'

He fixed me with another look out of the corners of his eyes. 'A right rum bit of paper, by the name on it; and a bit of paper that might well have fell out of the pocket of the said corpuss, him being a Frenchy.'

'We'll have your paper in a minute,' I said. 'When was the coach taken out? You'll recollect we were at the mortuary before eleven.'

'That's right,' the sharp little rascal agreed. 'And the coach was called for just gone nine; plenty of time for the job. Mr Gedge, the coachman, was sent for from the Two Chairmen, which is the mews tavern, him not in the best of tempers, not expecting to be called for before twelve o'clock, when he had to go and wait for Mr Dashwood at the House of Commons, the hosses was put in all of a hurry, and off they went with Mr Millichip and valet riding inside. Which likewise don't improve Mr Gedge's temper as he hates Mr Millichip's bowels.'

'No,' I announced. 'I don't believe it. I can't see any valet carrying away a corpse with its head blown off. It's not a thing a valet's commonly employed for. But what next?'

'What's next,' he continued, 'is that Mr Gedge himself comes down from the stable loft and says, "What are you nosing about for?" and I says, "Nothing", and he says, "You'd best take it and go then", so I reckon I'll put my head round the mews door to see how Jagger's getting on with Miss Polly Andrews and that scullery maid as you wanted him to give a shilling to. For my part I wanted to give her something else for misrepresenting me to the old besom. And if you want this bit of paper,' he added, cunningly, 'we'll have no more hard words about ladyship looking out and catching us all at it. Likewise, it's a hot day, and the hosses could do with a blow the same as Jagger and me could do with a pint of beer apiece for all our trouble.'

I gazed at him thoughtfully, turning over several things in my mind but also reflecting that it would be an opportunity for Jagger to make his own report, which he could not well do while driving. We were then approaching the pretty, pleasant purlieus of Islington Green and the old Queen's Head, the first stopping house for the York coaches where they are reputed to keep a very fair home brew, and there was no harm in a few minutes either way. Accordingly, I instructed Jagger that he might stop to enquire where Sadler's Walk may be and then, when we were settled in the

shade of an ancient elm tree with our pots before us, I said,
'Now then; this paper.'

It was a biggish and stiffish sheet folded into four, and it
must have fallen to the floor of the coach unseen as there was
a muddy heel mark stamped on one of the outer sides. When
I opened it out I perceived it was printed in heavy type, and
seemingly addressed to the Belgians, for it was headed 'The
Imperial Palace of Laeken, Brussels', but there was no date;
it was in French, which I shall here translate into our more
rational tongue, and it was the biggest piece of Goddamned
impudence I have ever seen in my life.

It said, 'Proclamation. The short-lived success of my
enemies detached you for a moment from my Empire: in my
exile on a rock in the sea I heard your complaints. The God
of Battles has decided the fate of your beautiful provinces:
Napoleon is among you. You are worthy to be Frenchmen.
Rise in mass, join my invincible phalanxes to exterminate
the remainder of those barbarians who are your enemies and
mine, for they fly with rage and despair in their hearts.
Napoleon.'

'Tasty, ain't it?' Maggsy enquired. 'He's a rare goer, that
Boney, ain't he?'

'He's a rare damned puffed-up bullfrog,' I said, torn
between an Englishman's natural anger at the insolence of
it, rude laughter at its temerity, and a fresh perplexity. But
seeing the look of ill-concealed triumph on Maggsy's face, as
if he had resolved our whole mystery, I said, 'It may mean
much or little. We don't know yet. But you did well to find
it.'

'My oath I did,' he asserted; 'And all you've got to do now
is to go and put the clappers on your Lady Dorothea and
that old besom, and I particular hope you clapper her, and

then ask 'em "What did you snitch that corpuss for, and where is he?" '

I shall confess that I was uneasy myself, but I cried, 'All I have to do, God help me, is to keep my patience with you. So be silent for a bit before the task gets too difficult. And let's have your report, Jagger,' I said. 'What have you got for me?'

'Why, precious little, guv'nor,' the good fellow answered. 'Save I'm certain sure there's something funny going on. I've never knowed Polly so flustered nor so fearful, or in such a hurry. And I could swear there was something on the tip of her tongue to tell me, but she daresn't say it.'

'It's the scullery wench I'm after,' I told him. 'Polly was with you in the peach house when the shot was fired, and I'm satisfied nobody got out past the pair of you. Nor past this little whelp at the front door. But somebody must have left the house, and the only other way is by the tradesmen's entrance and that skivvy. And she must have seen him.'

'No,' Jagger said positively. 'It's certain she never did. She ain't all that bright, and between me and Polly and a shilling we'd have had it out of her. She never see nobody.'

'Then be damned,' I demanded, 'where does that get us?'

'You know where it gets us as well as I do,' Maggsy announced shrilly. 'It's sticking out as plain as a pig's arse, but you don't want to see it. It gets us to somebody in the house. I keep telling you, they're all in it up to their snouts.' He fixed Jagger with an evil leer. 'And I wouldn't be surprised your Pretty Polly is as well.'

'Jagger,' I interposed to prevent fisticuffs from breaking out, 'let's get on to Sadler's Walk before I wring this creature's neck and save you the trouble.'

The Walk was an agreeable small countrified street, with a stretch of canal and line of trees to one side and a row of cottages to the other, each in its neat bit of garden and painted palings. A very proper retreat for a retired tutorial gentleman, as also was Number Nine behind Nottingham lace curtains and a varnished green door and brass knocker; and the little old woman who appeared almost as I lifted it seemed at first sight just of a part with all the rest. But I know my old ladies, all sorts and conditions of 'em, and there was no mistaking the sudden look of caution which descended on her face as she peered up at me. Without so much as giving me time to doff my beaver she said, 'Not today, thank you,' and made to shut the door in my face.

'No, ma'am,' I said, getting my foot in it, 'I've seen that trick before. I want a word or two with Doctor Slocombe, and I mean to have 'em.'

She tried a fresh tack then. 'Speak up,' she cried. 'I'm a bit hard of hearing.'

I am not commonly a man to lay ungentle hands on the ladies, but I had had more than enough tantrums from the fair sex for one day, and I was also aware of Maggsy and Jagger watching with some interest from the chaise. I was of no mood for further ceremony, and I bundled the old Jezebel inside before she knew what had got her, saying, 'Now, ma'am, we'll have no further nonsense. I'm from Bow Street, and I want Doctor Slocombe. So where is he?'

She considered me shrewdly for a minute and then replied, 'Bow Street, is it? You look too respectable for that lot. I thought you was a debt collector, or a husband or father. Or maybe a brother. But if you're Bow Street, I don't want no trouble. The doctor ain't here.'

'Then where is he?' I demanded in my most terrible voice.

'You don't have to shout,' she replied pettishly. 'I ain't deaf. As to where he is now, I don't just know; but he's gone to assassingate Boneyparte. And good riddance too, if you ask me.'

I gazed at her dumbfounded for a further minute before asking, 'He's gone to do what? You'll pardon me, ma'am,' I said politely, 'but you're cracked.'

'Not as cracked as some,' she replied, eyeing me with her head to one side. 'But have it as you please. I allus thought he had meant to go today; but seemingly he went last night.'

But I had the measure of the fantastical little dimity now, for these days the mention of Bow Street usually steadies 'em, and in my most benevolent manner I said, 'Why, then, ma'am, that's all I want to know. So seeing it's such a hot day why don't we just sit down a minute while you tell me about it.'

Thus encouraged I soon had the whole tale out of her, for what it was worth. Viz: that on the day before Doctor Slocombe had set out to attend Lady Dorothea's salon at two o'clock, meaning to walk to Hanover Square as he did not have the price of a hackney about him. Then, seeing as he had not returned by seven, Mrs Wildgoose—for such was her name—laid out a cold supper for him and took herself off to visit the Sadler's Wells Theatre in company with several other respectable ladies. Here the spectacle proved to be so uplifting and patriotic that several glasses of port wine were consumed in drinking confusion to Bonaparte; and when this entertainment was finished, the ladies next repaired to the house of one of their number, where some further loyal toasts were proposed in a particular fine old vintage elderberry.

Consequently, when Mrs Wildgoose returned at or about

midnight to her own domicile, finding it in darkness and feeling in some need of her own virtuous couch, she had concluded simply that Doctor Slocombe was safely at home and asleep. But on rising somewhat tardily this morning, and hastening to get his breakfast, she had discovered that, although he had eaten every vestige of his supper his bed had not been slept in, and there was no other sign of the said doctor. 'So he's gone to assassingate Boneyparte,' she finished. 'Like I said, I allus thought he was meant to go today, but seemingly he changed his mind.'

'That's what must have happened,' I agreed patiently. 'Well, it's a noble ambition. And did he take anything with him? Clothing and suchlike?'

'Couldn't go bare backside, could he?' she enquired. 'Had a valise packed ready. That's gone.'

'You're an uncommon sharp lady,' I told her. 'Now one more thing. You thought at first that I might be a husband or a father or a brother. Does that mean what I think it means?' I cocked one eyebrow at her to indicate that we both understood the ways of certain kinds of elderly gentlemen. 'A bit naughty with the ladies?'

'Naughty is, or naughty not,' she replied. 'I ain't saying no more nor that, though I've catched him looking at *me* very funny once or twice. But he's a wonderful walker for his age.'

'Yes,' I said, beginning to feel somewhat obscure again, and adding, 'You've been most obliging, ma'am, and I don't need to trouble you any more. But I shall have to look at his rooms for the mere formality.'

By now clearly taken by my kindly manner she raised no fresh objection to this and it was soon done, for there were only two. The bedchamber all orderly, and nothing to reveal whether he had left in a hurry or at leisure, by free will or otherwise. A few ancient garments still hanging in the clothes closet, the bed tidy, fresh candles in the candlesticks but one of 'em burned down about an inch, and the chamberpot not used. 'It's plain to see the doctor's fortunate in his lodging, ma'am,' I observed. 'Particular fortunate in having you to look after him. And now we'll just have a last quick look at his study.'

Neither did this tell me much more, however. Just as orderly, though somewhat fusty with the odour of the books which lined the most part of it, English, French, Latin and Greek, and many concerned with military campaigns and battles of one kind or another. Likewise, there was a neat pile of manuscript on the writing-table by the window, a mass of close writing superscribed on the first sheet: 'A Critical Consideration of Napoleon Bonaparte's Campaign in Russia in the year 1812, taken in some part from an Account of Captain Louis Fénelon, one time of the 12th Regiment of Chasseurs of the Imperial Army, by Erasmus Slocombe, M.A., D.D., Ph.D., D.Lit., etc.' The learned old goat was a regular war-horse, I mused, turning over the pages to see how far he had got with the work; which, no doubt, Lady Dorothea was paying for.

He had reached the point at which Bonaparte left his army in Russia, for in the few lines on the last page he had written: 'At this juncture the Emperor sent for his aide-de-camp, General Jean Rapp, and, as soon as Rapp entered, informed him, "I am leaving for Paris tonight. My presence there is essential for France, and for this unfortunate army." This disclosure greatly shocked Rapp, who had not been anticipating any such event, and he said, "I must advise you, Sire, that your departure will have an unpleasant effect on the troops: they are not expecting it," to which the

Emperor replied, "My return is essential." ' I mused briefly on this too, reflecting that it was odd for such an inveterate scribbler to break off so abruptly, but then turned my attention to the two drawers in the table.

At first sight there was nothing here of much account either; a bill or two for tobacco and snuff, a missive from a wine merchant, none too complimentary, a letter from a publisher whom I know to be a faithless rascal refusing Doctor Slocombe's kind offer of his work—and damnation fortunate for the Reverend Doctor in the end, could he but know it—another from Lady Dorothea referring to a new coat for the doctor, and then one more which brought me up sharp. Only a few words, and those fantastical, but written in the same backward sloping hand, with a broad-cut quill, as the nonsense doggerel I had discovered yesterday. They said: 'Dearest Philosopher: You may be assured that if you do as you propose I shall never speak to you again: Whereas if you do not I shall remain ever your loving Lasthenia.'

'So ho,' I said; but then perceiving that the old curiosity was about to protest against me rummaging in the doctor's drawers I hastened to add, 'A mere formality, ma'am; and I've near enough done. I wonder now, if you'd mind putting your head out of the street door to see whether my horses are getting restive?'

Thus reassured, the good, innocent soul trotted off as happy as a duck, and no sooner was her back turned than that note was safe in my inside pocket. Then, setting everything back as I had found it, I was out in the little shoebox of a hall to meet her as she returned announcing that all was well and my young men waiting for me most polite. 'So they should be, ma'am,' I observed. 'And once again I'm particular obliged, for there are those who take a kindly interest in the doctor and wish him well of his public-spirited ambition.' And then half out of the front door, as if on an afterthought, I said, 'But tell me one thing more, ma'am. How long has the doctor been with you?'

'Why, better of a year,' she answered promptly. 'And his lodging money always comes regular from Hanover Square.'

'Particular obliged,' I said yet again, making the dozen or so paces to the chaise in a hurry; and when Jagger asked smartly, 'Where to now, Guv'nor?' I replied, 'Bedlam, my lad; the madhouse. This business will have me there in the end, so I might as well go quiet now and be done with it. But we'll stop at the Queen's Head on the way and have a bite to eat first.'

In short I was much in need of a quiet study of the French language with my brisk little red-headed professor, Juliette; though she can be near enough Bedlam herself sometimes when she gets a tantrum on her. But first I related the oddities of Doctor Slocombe and Mrs Wildgoose to Maggsy and Jagger while we discussed a light dinner of a shoulder of salmon and a pigeon pie—this last being more bones and paste than pigeon—and afterwards gave them their further instructions. I should be about my own investigations for the afternoon, I said, and as a special favour they might have the chaise for themselves; at which Master Maggsy only half suppressed an uncommon wicked leer. They were to go back to Sadler's Walk, I told them, and by means of discreet inquiry find out whether or not a carriage had been noted outside Mrs Wildgoose's cottage just after dark last night.

That much done they were to return to London, take the letter I had discovered to our old screever, Holy Moses in

Seven Dials, and ask him what he could make of it. This, I will confess, was no more than a notion I had. The name Lasthenia was new to me, but I fancied it had a Latin or Greekish smack about it which Moses might recognise; for when the old rascal is sober he has a pretty fair learning himself, being a sometime parson who got defrocked because of trying to teach his squire's daughter one item not included in the Thirty Nine Articles. Next they were to proceed to the Bow Street office to learn if there was any further word of Major Finchingfield, or other fresh developments, and were finally to meet me at the Brown Bear by seven o'clock. And that, I concluded, would keep them pleasantly occupied for the afternoon. Then not withstanding a further evil leer from Maggsy I had Jagger call a hackney for me and gave the order for Rathbone Place, only stopping on the way to purchase a bottle or two of the champagne wine which Juliette affects; a beverage which never fails to inspire the dear creature, although I personally find it somewhat thin and belchiferous.

The niceties of that agreeable French lesson are my own business, but in the June heat my gallant trollop was not over-attired to start with and she was never one to wait on ceremony. Between the pair of us we soon had what little there was left down, revealing the naked truth, and then fell to study zestfully, with a lively consideration of conjugations, genders and several surprising declensions, on my part a hearty pressure of my observations and on hers a pretty, breathless clinch or two to show that she'd taken the point. Boney and his damned armies all forgotten, the mysteries of Hanover Square cast aside, and no thought of Master Maggsy roaming at large. But I should have known better.

It was coming up to five o'clock and we had drawn apart
for a truce, Juliette lying back on the day-bed like a spectacle
of Venus, somewhat damp and flushed from her expositions
and languidly fanning her tits with her chemise, while I
opened the next bottle of champagne to refresh ourselves
before embarking on a further consideration of the irregular
verbs. And all at once a thunder of feet on the stairs outside.
I knew on the instant what it was, for nobody in the world
could be so flat-footed as that evil monster. He seemed to
trip over something on the landing with a crash, fell against
the door and then set to hammering on it just as I got the
cork out of the bottle, and in my consternation and astonishment let the damned stuff spout all over Juliette's Seat of
Learning. She let out a screech that might have cracked the
windows, an observation that surprised even me, and
Master Maggsy bawled, 'Are you there, Sturrock? You get
out of her and into your britches, quick. You're wanted
urgent. Been a groom to and fro from Hanover Square to
Bow Street like a shuttlecock ever since two o'clock. And
there's this for you.'

So there was Juliette in a fine rage and all her naked glory,
dabbing at herself to mop up the fountain of wine and
shrieking most unlikely poetics, me snatching at my small
clothes and advising the wicked wretch what I would do
when I got my hands on him, and on the landing outside
fresh voices of the several other ladies lodging in the house.
From the clamour they, Juliette and Maggsy were making
between them they seemed to think it was a riot, and I could
not get out to reassure them for fear of further excitement
from the sight of all my Worldly Goods so largely displayed,
while Maggsy screeched, 'Not bloody likely,' to one of my
promises. 'You have a look at this first,' he added. On that a

letter appeared under the door, and his boots began to
clump off down the stairs, only pausing as he bawled back,
'I've got the chaise waiting. And I've got information;
special and particular. So you go easy if you want to get it.'

By now growing tired of Juliette's unladylike observations
I awarded the pretty baggage a hearty slap on the rump to
quieten her, then set to dragging on my pantaloons with one
hand and snatching up the letter with the other, now
perceiving that it was addressed in Lady Dorothea's writing
and marked, 'Most urgent and in haste'. And when I got it
open, half in my shirt, it continued, 'Mr Sturrock; Sir: I
much regret that we last parted on a note of mutual
misunderstanding. You will appreciate, however, that we
have suffered several Distracting Anxieties of late, and there
is now added another to these. Your immediate attention
and advice is most earnestly desired, and in confidence of
this kindness I am your most obliged Dorothea Hookham-
Dashwood.'

'Short and sweet,' I observed, 'but what have we now, I
wonder? My love,' I added to the blushing Juliette, giving
her tits a final squeeze for consolation, 'I can hardly bear to
tear myself away from our studies, but I have other occasions calling me.'

Four

Jagger was waiting for me by the horses with his face as straight as a ramrod, and Master Maggsy peering from behind him giving me another mongrel look out of the corners of his eyes. 'Here,' he started, 'you lay off. You want to gut anybody, you save it for old Abel Makepenny, for he set me to find you. "Double quick", says he, "and no matter what." Which I done. And I got some damnation rummy information what you ought to have before we stop by Hanover Square, but if you come anything with me I shall skip and you won't get it.'

'It had better be important,' I said, bundling him into the chaise and adding to Jagger. 'Make it as quick as you can, my lad.'

'It's rummy anyway,' he replied, still warily keeping as far away from me as he could, 'and we shan't be all that quick neither, for the traffic's wicked again.'

In that at least the wretch spoke the truth, for there was fresh excitement abroad with the newsboys crying that Boney's armies were over the Belgian frontier, and crowds snatching at their sheets, while we had scarcely turned into Oxford Street when all vehicles were halted and cleared to the side to make way for a squadron of Light Dragoons and a string of their horses trotting past. But I had no thought that we ourselves were already on our way to seeing these fine fellows in action, and I replied. 'Be damned to the traffic. Let me have your report, you cross-eyed whelp, while I decide whether to break your head or your neck.'

'Item,' Maggsy began hurriedly, 'and the least first. Ain't been no word of Major Finchingfield at Bow Street today. Old Abel Makepenny just about got that much out before he hustled me off to fetch you.'

'I'm not so sure that that is the least,' I answered. 'But get on.'

'The second,' he continued, 'as to that letter I took to Holy Moses. He was fair to middling sober, and he says he dunno what the letter means, but otherwise for how much it's worth to you there was some philosopher once named Plato, and his favourite lady pupil was named Lasthenia. I personally never heard of the cove myself, but if he was anything like this Doctor Slocombe I can guess a good bit about him.'

'So ho,' I mused. 'And likewise a damned good guess on my part to send it to Moses. I begin to see one glimmer of light. And what of Sadler's Walk?'

'There's the nub of it,' Maggsy announced. 'And that town and country kerridge. I keep telling you that the Hanover Square lot is up to their snouts in mischief. There's a woman two doors down from Mrs Wildgoose, a Mrs Peabody, as inquisitive as a ferret and her eyes stuck on stalks. Well, then, a bit after half gone nine last night she hears a kerridge come up with a trot and a jingle and stop by Mrs Wildgoose's, and thinking it might be another gentleman come to have a word or two with the doctor about his little games, she peers through the curtains to see what's what.

But it ain't a gentleman gets out, it's an old lady, who gives a rattle bang on the door as if she's in an uncommon sharp temper.'

'Don't let your fancies run away with you again, boy,' I warned him. 'There are thousands of sharp old ladies in London, just as there are thousands of town and country coaches.'

'Wait till you hear the rest of it,' he answered. 'It being a fine warm night Mrs Peabody then reckons to take a little walk to see what she can hear, but when she comes abaft the kerridge the coachman gives her a wicked dirty look, and she steers off to watch from across the street under the trees. Whereupon she sees the doctor come out pretty well at a trot and carrying a valise, the old lady hustling him on, calling him a damned old fool, and pretty well shoving him into the kerridge. And, what's more, as she gets in herself she calls up to the aforesaid coachman and says. "We've a long way to go, Gedge, so don't dawdle about it." There might be thousands of old ladies about,' the obstinate creature finished, 'and there might be thousands of town and country kerridges, but I'll lay odds there ain't all that many coachmen named Gedge.'

I was forced to admit that it was a curious circumstance, but I added, 'None the less it disposes of your crackpot theory that it was the Hanover Square carriage which carried off Captain Fénelon's body.'

'Looks like it,' he admitted unwillingly, 'though it's a pity. I had a fancy for that notion; that old besom sitting and clutching an horrid corpuss with half his head blowed off.'

'Be careful, you rascal,' I warned him. 'You're not out of danger yet. I've still got an itchy finger on my cane, so keep to your story. In short, where was the valet, Millichip? You said this morning that he came out to the carriage in the mews last night; then they'd have gone round to the front door for Miss Harriet to get in. But where was he when they got to Sadler's Walk?'

'Dunno,' Maggsy replied indifferently. 'The old cluck, Peabody, was certain sure she only see Mr Gedge and the old besom. Might've been sitting in the dark in the kerridge,'

'And let a lady get out first?' I enquired. 'Not if he's got the genteel manners a valet should have. This Mr Millichip seems to disappear and reappear pretty well at pleasure. Yesterday at the time of the unfortunate occurrence Miss Harriet declares he's nowhere to be found. Next he appears in the mews about nine o'clock. Then he's gone again in Sadler's Walk. But we shall have to look into that later with this fresh trouble on our hands. Was there any word of what it is?'

'Not as I know of,' Maggsy said. 'If the Hanover Square groom told Abel Makepenny, Abel was in too much of a hurry to tell me. I wouldn't be surprised of another corpuss. We shall find out soon enough.'

'If we ever come out of this damned confusion,' I observed as we got into a fresh thick of traffic, hemmed in by a brewer's dray and a market cart and several others, compliments abounding, and all tangling into the side again to let a fresh troop of cavalry horses come riding down hell for lick.

We were fortunate to get into the peace of Hanover Square without losing at least a wheel, as well as our patience; and they were watching out for us anxiously at the house, for no sooner had I got down from the chaise than the door was opened by Miss Harriet herself, who announced, 'Ye've been long enough about it, my man. We sent our first message for yer before two o'clock.'

'Miss Harriet,' I replied, 'at two o'clock I was attending to other duties; and have been all the afternoon. My affairs ain't all tea-parties and philosophy.'

'Fiddlesticks,' she rejoined. 'And come down off your high horse. Dorothea's waiting for you in the morning room.'

'Then I shall be pleased to attend on her,' I said. 'But first I could do with knowing what it's all about. Nobody's told me yet.'

'Simple enough,' Miss Harriet snapped. 'Georgina's vanished, the little hussy. Her and that saucy maid of hers, both upped and gone. Dorothea told the fellow we sent for you not to say too much, as we don't want it talked of all over the town.' And both thought I would not come for such a trifling matter, I reflected shrewdly, as she marched across to fling open the morning room door and announce, 'Here he is, Dorothea; at long last.'

My lady greeted me with her kindest smile, so making it plainer still that our little disagreement was now quite forgotten, and I was too much a gentleman to observe that it is a delicate art of the ladies to be all forgiveness when they want a favour. 'I cannot say how grateful we are,' she protested sweetly, 'Miss Harriet has told you of our latest anxiety?'

'A mere mention, ma'am,' I replied. 'Not in any great detail.'

'There is very little detail to add,' she said, and proceeded to tell the tale. The first thing this morning Miss Harriet had gone into the chit's bedchamber to enquire after her health, but she had complained of still feeling swoonish and begged to be allowed to lie abed until midday. Thereupon the maid Polly had taken up her breakfast a little after nine; and, according to the kitchen, an uncommon hearty breakfast for a swoonish young lady. Then Miss Harriet had gone to the room again at half past twelve—'To have her out of it smartish, fits and vapours or not,' the old lady interjected—and thereby discovered her absence. Finally the gardener's boy, Alfred, had somewhat belatedly confessed that he had observed a servant's wicker travelling basket in one of the peach houses, seemingly secreted there some time last night.

'Undoubtedly paid to keep his mouth shut,' I observed. 'And I have my own information that the woman, Polly, was somewhat hurried and agitated this morning.'

'Prying again?' Miss Harriet enquired, cocking a sharp eye at me. 'Shall I have that demned boy fetched in, Dorothea?' she asked.

'There's no need,' Lady Dorothea answered sharply. 'He cannot tell us any more than we already know. We are wasting time,' she added to me. 'It is quite clear that Georgina has gone to Brussels. The means and the method do not matter. I desire you to go there to find her, Mr Sturrock.'

I gazed at her in open astonishment. Even for a titled lady that was somewhat tall; and I thought swiftly that if this disappearance were connected with one or two other small matters I could mention, the means and method might be a damned sight more important than she realised. But I could also see the way to a nice little bargain here if I handled it cleverly; as I commonly handle these things. 'Ma'am,' I said, 'I ask nothing better than to serve you. But that I can't do.'

'And why not, pray?' she demands, sharper than ever.

'A matter of duty, ma'am,' I explained. 'Head of Bow Street Force as I may be, I still have my masters. I should have to ask for leave of absence, at least a week or more, and in times like these our Chief Magistrate would never grant it. It grieves me to say it,' I continued, 'but he would never consider the elopement of a somewhat wild young lady—for that's what it looks like—warrant enough to lose the service of his first officer for so long.'

Lady Dorothea gave me a curious and unreadable look. 'So you have heard of that foolish affair at Hookham Priors? And you think of it as simply as that?'

'Unless you can tell me anything different, ma'am,' I suggested, very soft.

I had a fair notion that under her appearance of calm my lady was pretty near distracted, and there was a quick glance between her and Miss Harriet, but she answered, 'No, I cannot.'

'Then that's a pity,' I mused. 'For, if I could advise my chief that Miss Georgina's disappearance may be part of some graver matter, I fancy he'd tell me to get on with it quick.'

Lady Dorothea paused again. 'You are referring to Captain Fénelon?'

'We're taking an interest in the late gentleman at Bow Street,' I admitted. 'And it's certain that Mr Masters might tell us something. Has he spoken yet?'

'He has not,' Miss Harriet snapped. 'Not a word you can make sense of. Only some kind of "Mm . . . mm . . ." '

'So he wants to say something?' I demanded, sharpish myself.

'Mr Sturrock,' my lady interrupted, 'understand once and for all that I will not have Masters troubled. Our physician says that if there is to be any hope of recovery he is to have absolute quiet. That is the end of the matter.'

I bowed to her politely, keeping my patience. 'As you wish, ma'am. Though even at the cost of Miss Georgina?'

'You know as well as I do that you can find Georgina without killing Masters,' she cried angrily.

'You have a kind faith in my abilities,' I said. 'But allow me to turn to Captain Fénelon. Will you tell me what he was doing here yesterday?'

She seemed to hesitate, either for something she was hiding or because she truly did not know. 'He arrived here a little before the other gentlemen, and when I expected him to join us at tea he begged to be excused. He asked to be allowed to remain in the waiting-room, where he proposed to write an account of something. This, he said, he would then leave with me; though requesting me to keep it sealed until certain events should seem to make it advisable to open it. He particularly asked my word on that.'

'Oh, be damned,' I exclaimed irritably. 'The fellow's too much a man of mystery. He ain't natural.' But then recovering my politeness I enquired, 'And did you ever have or see this writing?'

'I did not,' she answered. 'Indeed I quite forgot it in the events of yesterday. I did not think of it again until . . .'

She stopped, and I finished for her, 'Until Miss Georgina disappeared today.' It was very plain there was something they were still not telling me, but I now had a fair idea of what it was. Beginning to lose my patience with the pair of 'em, I hauled off on a fresh tack to lay a shot from an unexpected quarter, and addressed myself to Miss Harriet. 'Tell me, now, if you will, where did Doctor Slocombe get out of your coach last night and then get in again some time after the rain started?'

It took both of 'em close hauled; an instant of dumbfoundment, while they gazed at each other and then at me, before Miss Harriet exclaimed, 'Well, be demned, how d'you know that, you rascal?', looked at Lady Dorothea again, announced, 'He might as well be told,' and finished, 'At the Saracen's Head in Beaconsfield, for what that may mean to you. Late as it was, the place was still lit up, having some cavalrymen riding from the village, and the demned old fool wanted to relieve himself. I told him to get down and fetch a glass of brandy apiece for me and him and Gedge.'

'What it means to me,' I explained kindly, 'is that Beaconsfield ain't far from Hookham Priors. Where you took the Reverend Doctor Slocombe last night to keep him out of mischief. Which you decided upon in a hurry after confronting Miss Georgina with that nonsense doggerel I found in the waiting-room yesterday. The same doggerel, as you were quick to perceive, Miss Harriet, being written in the young lady's hand.'

'Well, be demned,' the old lady repeated, 'how the devil do you know that as well?'

'A further note the little fool—the young lady sent to the reverend gentleman; in which I fancy she warned him that if he disclosed anything she would never speak to him again. I fancy the gentleman is somewhat foolish about her, and she knows it. She addresses him as "Philosopher" and refers to herself as his "Lasthenia". A little classical learning will make the allusion clear, ma'am,' I added modestly to Lady Dorothea, who was gazing at me as goggle-eyed as the nobility can ever allow themselves to get. 'But why,' I demanded. 'why in heaven's name did you not tell me of this fantastical plot at once and save so much questioning?'

By the look of her Miss Harriet was about to come up with a sharpish answer, but Lady Dorothea interjected, 'No,

Harriet, we'll have no more cross-purposes. We did not learn about it ourselves until last night, Mr Sturrock; and thought it was scotched until Georgina's absence was discovered today. Then we concluded that it seems so nonsensical, so inconceivably missish and silly, that you would merely laugh at the matter and refuse to act.'

'Nonsensical, missish and inconceivable it is,' I agreed. 'And the little fool wants her arse slapping.' I amended myself quickly. 'The young lady needs some very severe correction. But it's also damnation dangerous. I shall not trouble you with several more matters which seem to be connected with it, ma'am, for you've got enough vexations on your plate already. I'll say only that there seem to be several other people taking too much interest. In short, it looks as if Miss Georgina's started something she can't stop.'

'Mr Sturrock,' she demanded, 'Will you, or will you not go after her?'

'I will,' I answered without more ado. In fact I now perceived that it was the only way I should get at the whole truth, as well as probably saving the little slut's life—for what that was worth. 'And I'd go tonight if it were possible,' I continued, 'but I don't see how that's to be done. My own horses will scarcely get me to Harwich. And there's the question of funds. At this hour my bank is closed and won't open for business again until the morning.'

I paused, and Lady Dorothea rose to the bait like the imperious nobility she is. 'That's of no consequence. Our carriage and Gedge are at your disposal. And we can arrange quite sufficient funds to start with.'

'Very good,' I said. 'Then have your carriage come to the Brown Bear in Drury Lane by a little after seven. I'm bound to go there myself to arrange certain matters and send a message for the Chief Magistrate. Then we'll try to intercept her before she sails, for here's how I see it. If we say she left about twelve she can hardly get to Harwich before ten tonight, and it's doubtful if she'll find a packet leaving as late as that. She'll have to find an inn and wait until the morning, and with good fortune we may be there ourselves by then. Now, ma'am,' I finished, 'There's a few more questions before I get on my way; and I'll thank you to answer 'em straight and plain. First; has Miss Georgina got any funds?'

'She will be a very considerable heiress eventually,' Lady Dorothea said. 'But she should not have anything with her now. Young ladies do not need to carry money.'

I nodded. 'So she's got confederates. And that young fellow from Hookham Priors, Tom Debenham, comes to mind. Do you know what regiment he's in, and whether he's already in Belgium?'

'The last I cannot say,' my lady replied. 'But he is an ensign in the Fifty-Second Oxfordshire Infantry.'

'And probably already in the line by now,' I mused. 'Which leaves us Captain ffoulkes. Cavalrymen don't commonly have much truck with infantry, regarding 'em as a lower form of animal, but it's possible he might know Debenham. Captain ffoulkes lodges in Portland Place. Have you thought to enquire there?'

This time it was Miss Harriet's turn. 'First thing we did, you blockhead. Young ffoulkes' grandmother's place. Known Kitty Beddoes all me life, and we speak our minds to each other. The boy got his hosses and left in a demnition hurry; likewise about midday. Kitty swears she saw no sign of the wenches, and I believe her; but it's sticking out as plain as the nose on your face.'

'So it would seem,' I agreed. 'Now there's one last thing. The valet, Mr Millichip. He got into your carriage in the mews last night, but he does not seem to have gone as far as Sadler's Walk. Do you know where he was bound for and what he was doing?'

Her ladyship stared at me in fresh astonishment. 'For pity's sake, Mr Sturrock,' she cried, 'what are you thinking of now? Millichip was merely sent to carry a message to my husband at the House of Commons. The carriage was to take him as far as the hackney stand in Oxford Street, where he was to engage a hackney.'

'It's only that I like to have everything explained,' I said. 'And I'll not overtax your patience any longer now. If I don't overtake the young lady at Harwich I'll go on to Brussels,' I promised; but I felt it kinder not to add to their present anxieties by telling them why.

I have spoken of the Brown Bear also on several other occasions, and shall say little more of it now. A low place, but a convenient rendezvous for such rascals as sometimes bring me information and would not dare to show their ugly faces in the Bow Street office; likewise One-Eyed Jack, the landlord, knows which side his bread is buttered on and keeps a very respectable claret for me at a reasonable price—all of it smuggled, though now getting short again owing to Master Bonaparte's antics, and another good reason for getting this damned war done with. But at the early hour of seven o'clock the place was respectable enough, for the whoring and fighting does not commonly start until somewhat later, and the only villain of note present was Slippery Solomon, the receiver, sitting like a Hebrew prophet with a watchful eye on our Bow Street man,

Burchall; who, it will be recollected, had been sent out by Abel Makepenny about further inquiries.

Being somewhat earlier than I anticipated I had left Maggsy and Jagger at our chambers to put up the chaise, stable the horses and pack bags for all three of us, while I walked through the crowded streets to Drury Lane—where the rumours and excitement were rising alike hour by hour—half expecting to find Major Finchingfield also waiting for me, and considering how I should conduct my inquiries with Burchall if he were there. Fortunately however, Burchall was alone, and with some relief I said, 'Well met, Andrew, and you're timely. Which is just as well, as I'm off to Harwich and very likely Ostend and Brussels as soon as may be.'

'So ho,' he observed, for the saucy rogue sometimes affects to copy some of my own manners, 'sooner you than me the way things look. They say the news is worse than ever.'

'It gets worse every day,' I agreed. 'so you can call for a pot of claret for me and we'll get to business.'

Somewhat chastened by that he rapped on the table to fetch the serving wench, pushed his beaver to the back of his head and continued, 'As to business, there ain't any. We're troubled with a plague of disappearances.'

'I've noticed that phenomenon myself,' I nodded. 'But who in particular this time?'

'Your Major Finchingfield, for one,' he announced. 'I was at the King's Arms not an hour since, the whole place in an uproar, crying out for horses, dispatching everything they've got on wheels, and the landlord more than a bit above himself. I was bound to talk a bit of Bow Street sense to him, but he came out plain enough in the end. What it amounts to is that if this major merely posted he wouldn't know him, as they've had dozens of officers passing through. Contrariwise, however, if the major had lodged there he would. And he don't.'

'Be damned,' I exclaimed, 'that's another facer. Are you sure of it?'

'Ain't I always sure?' he asked. 'There's been no Major Finchingfield lodged at the King's Arms either last night or any other night. Now as to the Captain Fénelon,' he went on, not without a certain relish, 'he's another that appears to be very likewise. As you're aware, there ain't so many émigrés about now, and I've been after one or another of 'em all day. But if any of 'em knows Fénelon or knows of him, they're keeping uncommon quiet. To be sure,' he added, 'I might have missed something. Though I doubt it.'

'It's damned certain you've missed something,' I retorted, warmly. 'I've got half a dozen witnesses who can swear to him.'

'I'd say he don't exist,' Burchall said doggedly. 'But for one thing. You recollect old Christophe? Been here since before the Terror in '93. Calls himself a dancing master, but panders for one or two knocking shops on the Haymarket and does a trade in country girls with 'em when he gets the chance.'

'Andrew,' I told the fellow benevolently, 'I was interrogating Christophe Lebaume before you ever thought of joining the Force.'

'So you'll know that commonly butter wouldn't melt in his mouth,' he continued unabashed. 'But he was edgy when I put the Bow Street touch on him today. Well, then, I got a bit out of him that might mean your Captain Fénelon, and it's plain there's something in the wind. And at the Grecian Coffee House, as you advised,' he conceded handsomely. 'In short, a pretty regular meeting of three there. One thick-set and about middle-aged, but otherwise a description that might fit anybody; the other somewhat younger and of a gentlemanly manner, but no better description; and both of these unknown to Cristophe. The third, however, a certain Joseph Coignet who *is* known to him. They're always talking low-voiced in French, and several times Cristophe tries to get in with 'em, only to be told to take himself off. And he swears that he never caught any snatch of their conversation; but he's lying, for it's damned certain that he's nervous about something.'

I carefully refrained from saying 'So ho', and observed instead, 'We might be getting on the track a bit, Andrew.'

'We might,' he agreed. 'And if your Captain Fénelon does exist he might be the fellow of a gentlemanly manner, for by what little more I can get out of Christophe it seems he's seen signs of strong disagreement between him and the other two once or twice. So I conclude that as it's no use looking for two unknown and nondescript men I'll go after this Joseph Coignet; and under further pressure Cristophe admits that I might get more information about him either from Sims' theatrical Agency at the Harp Tavern, or the Hog in the Pound off Oxford Street.'

'The Hog in the Pound,' I mused, and then exclaimed, 'Hold your horses a minute, Andrew. The Hog in the Pound, not a stone's throw from Hanover Square and kept by Bully Wheeler, one time stagecoach driver and reputed to run anything that got in his way off the road. And Bully Wheeler also keeps a four-in-hand which he hires out to the sporting fraternity to go to race meetings and boxing matches and suchlike.'

'You know 'em all, don't you?' Mr Burchall enquired.

'Well, then, I went to Sims' Agency first but had no good there, for it was closed for the day, and then on to the Hog. And little better there except that Wheeler was as innocent as a virgin, started by swearing that he'd never heard of Coignet, and then declared that he hadn't seen him for some several weeks past.'

'By God, Wheeler'd make a pretty virgin,' I cried. 'You've earned your pay today, Andrew, for what little it is. Now here's what I want you to do; and do it quick. Arrest him tonight on charges of aiding and abetting in the removal of a corpse from Mary-le-bone mortuary, and accessory before the murder of the man Wilkes. Likewise arrest Cristophe. You can make that what you like; procuring country girls'll do for a start. Then sweat the blood out of both of 'em.' I stopped as a sudden fresh thought struck me. 'Come to think of it, Miss Georgina could be called a country girl; and such things have been done. But it'd need cool rogues to dare that. Be damned, this puts us in a most particular quandarious position, Andrew. We might have the nub of it under our fingers here; yet I'm bound to go to Harwich, and maybe Brussels, to look after that end.'

Burchall made no reply at first, only emptying his pot and putting it down somewhat pointedly before observing, 'I ain't just exactly a new-born babe.'

'My God, you ain't,' I agreed, banging on the board to call the wench. 'No more'n Bully Wheeler's a virgin. And no new-born babe could suck claret like that. It's plain we must split forces; so you'd best hear all of it, or as much as I know myself.'

So saying, I embarked on a quick recital, while the good fellow said nothing, only nodding now and again, or grunting or taking a fresh pull at his drink for a change, until I concluded, 'So there you have it. A damned old fool of a tutor up to his ears in military matters and doting on young girls; a French officer who was reputed to have his own grudge against Boney; and this romantic miss who probably propounded the whole crackpot plot. And others by the look of it; for somebody must be funding 'em as they don't have any money of their own. Where the two boys come in I'm not sure, but I fancy young ffoulkes has been persuaded it's a simple runaway to get to this Tom Debenham in Brussels and he's merely escorting her there. From what I've heard of her that little devil could twist Satan's tail round her middle finger.'

Burchall said nothing for a minute, but then he asked, 'It ain't such a crackpot notion, though, is it? Given an officer who knows his way around in the French army and a uniform, which wouldn't be all that hard to come by, it might even be pretty easy on the battlefield. And it'd save everybody a lot of trouble. She's a rare flyer, this Miss Georgina, ain't she?'

'It might be pretty easy,' I retorted, 'if the fool who did it was prepared to lose his own life on the instant after. And nobody can tell me that Captain Fénelon was so cracked that he didn't see that.'

'No,' he agreed, pondering the point. 'It don't add up, do it?' he asked. 'And who's the other party; the one who's providing the money?'

'Andrew,' I confessed, 'there's several things I don't know what to make of. And three to be getting on with are our mysterious major, how Boney's proclamation came to be in the Hanover Square carriage—though that was most likely dropped by the Reverend Slocombe, and don't seem to be all that important—and Miss Georgina's nonsense doggerel.'

'As to the last,' he observed with some care, 'I'd say you might have asked the ladies.'

'I might have done, but I didn't,' I said shortly. 'For one thing, they was near enough distracted already; for another, there wasn't time; and, for one more, I've a notion to reckon that little puzzle out myself. And by the look of it, we don't have much more time ourselves now,' I added, for Master Maggsy and Jagger with our bags had now appeared at the door, plainly as pleased as dogs with two tails at the thought of the jaunt before us.

They were followed close after by Mr Gedge and another fellow—though I did not take much note of this one at first—and I finished to Burchall, 'Now, Andrew, you must go fast tonight. Arrest Cristophe Labaume and Bully Wheeler. Find this Joseph Coignet if you can; or if you can't, go to the Sims Agency first thing tomorrow. I want to know what business he has there. And I want the information sent after me, so go to Hanover Square and tell Lady Dorothea that I must have your report. There's plenty of money on hand and she'll not stint it; she'll send a special courier if you use your wits the right way. As to myself, I shall try to catch the little trollop before she boards the Ostend packet, and then your messenger may meet us on the road coming back. If not, I'll contrive to leave word of my movements at the Harbour Master's office. It's bound to be hit or miss, but I must have that information, and I don't care how you get it to me.'

There was no time for more as by now Mr Gedge, Jagger and Maggsy was all about us and Burchall nodded, as quick in the uptake as most, as I said, 'You're in good time, Mr Gedge; and just as well, for we must go fast.'

Gedge and myself were pretty well known to each other,

and mostly of a cordial manner, but tonight he seemed not in the best of tempers, glancing sideways at the other fellow, still standing close behind him. 'That's as may be,' he answered. 'It's a long pull, and from all I hear it'll be none too easy to get a change of horses on the road. But her ladyship bid me place these in your hands, and to say she's thankful to you and wishes you Godspeed.'

So saying he produced several items, the first and most gratifying being a fine heavy purse, which I stowed away on the instant in my back pocket, and the others three sealed packets; one marked 'Letter of Credit', the next addressed to me, and the last to a Lady Georgiana Lennox; this also being gratifying as a sign that we were still to move in the most genteel circles. 'And we've brought your pistols,' Master Maggsy announced. 'I reckon we shall want 'em before this lot's done with.'

'Indeed I hope not, sir,' the other man behind Gedge observed. 'I am exceedingly nervous in the presence of firearms,' he added, while Gedge gave him another sideways look like a mischancy horse contemplating landing you a kick in the guts with its left hind hoof; which quietly disregarding the fellow continued as bland as barley water, 'Millichip, sir. Ambrose Millichip, personal gentleman to Mr Dashwood.'

'Indeed,' I observed, gazing at him and reflecting briefly that by the look of him he would not be all that nervous in the presence of anything. Neat and spick as a valet should be with a sober frockcoat very near as well cut as my own, though somewhat tanned about the face for an indoor servant, as they commonly run pale and weedy; and something about him which struck a notion in me that I'd seen him before somewhere. But I could not place the occasion on the instant, and I asked. 'Well now, Mr Millichip, what can we do for you?'

'For Mr Dashwood, sir,' he amended. 'Mr Dashwood wishes to express his concern in this matter, and desires me to travel with you in the hope that I may be of some small assistance. If it be convenient.'

Still gazing at him I replied. 'Which is very civil of him, and I don't see any particular inconvenience,' though Gedge looked as if he did, as black as thunder with it, and I said, 'So ho,' soft to myself and continued, 'So you'd best ride inside. You can get up on the box with Mr Gedge, Jagger, and take a turn with the ribbons if he feels like asking you. And you, Maggsy, put the bags in the boot and let's get started.'

Then while they were all about that bustle I drew Burchall aside, saying softly, 'There's another commission for you, Andrew. I've no reason to doubt that Mr Millichip ain't exactly what he seems to be, but I've no reason to believe that he is; and he's another one who disappears and appears at pleasure. I want you to go to the House of Commons; they're generally still at their wrangling and hullabaloo pretty late. Get one of the ushers or the clerk of the Lobby and find out what time a message was sent into the Chamber for Mr John Dashwood last night; and what it was, if you can. And then, if you've any time to spare, you might do worse than look around some of the whore shops Cristophe Labaume panders for; see what you can pick up there.'

He made a remarkably coarse reply, which I shall not repeat, neither did I answer it myself, but turned away to climb into the coach and give the order to advance. So, having cast a net in several directions, and hoping to God it would catch something, we set off at last to the accompaniment of several cheers and other comments from the urchins and rude bystanders gathered around.

Five

There was still some daylight left, and while Gedge turned eastwards to the City—where the excitement was still rising and the newsboys bawling fresh reports—to pass out through Bow on the Colchester road, I opened Lady Dorothea's note addressed to me. Like the good lady herself it was plain, simple and no frills on it, but of a most spacious nobility, for it said, 'Mr Sturrock; Sir: I need hardly express how deeply obliged we are. If you are forced to travel so far, as I fear you may be, I add here a letter of introduction to my friend Lady Georgiana Lennox, who is the daughter of the Duke and Duchess of Richmond, to whom I have explained your mission and your kindness. The Richmonds have been resident in Brussels for close on a year, and I have no doubt they will be pleased to open such doors for you as you may find it useful to enter. The purse Gedge will hand to you contains one hundred pounds for current disbursement, but in the event of your requiring further funds I have provided also a letter of credit which I have requested the Duke to honour with his own banker in Brussels. Pray spare no necessary expense; and, believe me, your obliged, etc . . .'

In short, a most genteel epistle; more particularly the instruction to pray spare no expense. I may add also that it was the means by which I was present at the Duchess of Richmond's famous ball on the Eve of Waterloo; when, as the poet says, 'The lamps shone o'er fair women and brave men'. But that is getting a bit ahead of my tale, and will appear in its due place; though, had I then known of the fearful scenes and dangers which lay before us, I might well have been tempted to leave Miss Georgina Wilde-Hookham to her own fanciful devices and put my head out of the window to order Gedge to turn back to London uncommon quick.

As it was, however, I found myself fretting with impatience at the worthy fellow keeping his horses to a gentle trot, while every other damned horseman and curricle, phaeton or chaise passed us in a rattle and clatter, all making towards Harwich, and some of the impudent rascals even bawling at us to give way. I could hardly expect him to match the reckless speed of the flying stagecoaches, ten miles an hour or more, yet at this pace we had little hope of arriving before long after the first morning packet had sailed, and it was as much as I could do to restrain myself from calling up to him to touch up his leaders a bit. But, as many a lady has discovered to her cost, it is a dangerous thing to argue with the driver if you wish to get to your destination intact and with all your skirts still round your ankles, and I kept silent though it was a choleric effort. Resolving to have Jagger on the ribbons the first change we got, I turned to a contemplation of the valet, sitting opposite in the other corner, and at last announced, 'Mr Millichip, I'm certain sure I've seen you before some time.'

'Have you indeed, sir?' he enquired politely. 'Perhaps at Lord Bettsford's establishment. I was with my lord before entering Mr Dashwood's service.'

Considering I did not know my Lord Bettsford from Adam I concluded that was somewhat unlikely, and said only, 'Let it pass; it's no great importance. It'll come to me in the end, for I never forget a face.'

But before I could persue the matter further there was another clatter of hoofs racing up close behind us, some scoundrel roaring, 'Road, there; give way you damned idlers,' a chaise coming up hard and fast, shaving so close that we very near lost our offside wheel caps, Gedge cursing soulfully and using his whip on the rascals to drive 'em clear, and the horses snorting and rearing as bad as a calvalry charge. I thought we were like to have gone arse over tip into the ditch, but with Jagger hurling sundry further compliments after him the dastardly pirate broke away somehow, and by the time Master Maggsy had finished his unlovely observations and Gedge had got our own team in step again the question of where I had seen Mr Millichip before was quite forgotten. Whether he was relieved or not by that I do not know, but after seeming both amused and startled by Maggsy's poetics he was quick to seize on a fresh subject. 'It was certainly murderous driving,' he agreed. 'Road manners get worse every day.'

'Be damned to road manners,' I answered. 'If Gedge were to put a touch of pace on and keep up with the other traffic we should all be a good bit safer. He's nursing his cattle as if they're the last he'll ever see.'

'It may be that he thinks they are,' Mr Millichip said. 'I understand that he fears it may be difficult to effect changes. I myself read in *The Times* this morning that all the post houses on the Dover and Harwich roads are at their wits' end for fresh horses.' He paused for a minute on that and then enquired, 'May I be permitted to make a suggestion?'

'If it'll get us to Harwich any quicker I shall be damned glad of it,' I told him.

'It might do,' he promised. 'As you no doubt know, sir, the proper place for a first change should be the George at Brentwood. But as the roads are tonight it seems extremely unlikely that they'll oblige us. I would propose we try the Plough instead. It's a smaller house, and not so well known, but they have a very fair stable, and I feel sure we shall do better there. Indeed, if you care to leave the matter to me I think I can arrange it. I might also add that they keep a good table if you wish to take supper.'

'Begod,' I cried, 'you're a very mine of information, Mr Millichip.'

'I try to do my best, sir,' he replied modestly. 'My Lord Bettswood has his country seat near Earl's Colne, and I have travelled this road with him on several occasions.' He gave a little cough on that, and then added, 'If I might further suggest, sir, it would be as well if this proposal seemed to come from you to Mr Gedge rather than from myself. I do not understand why he should, but Mr Gedge has a certain animus against me.'

'Coachmen, Mr Millichip.' I said jovially. 'You know what they are. They're all as tetchy and uncertain as their horses.'

I sat regarding him with some benevolence, for I must now reveal what I have so far kept dark; namely, that I had known for some time past what that rhyming doggerel was. Not what it meant, as plainly the nonsense words could not have any meaning, but what it was for. The thought had come to me in a single light of inspiration—such as I frequently enjoy—and here, I reflected, might be a chance of putting it to the test; and if it failed we should be no worse off. So when the darkness was gathering about us and Gedge hauled on his ribbons to pull up the coach, announcing a stop to light the lamps, I got out myself saying, 'And I'll take the opportunity for a quiet piss; and you'd best come too, Maggsy. And you, Jagger,' I called up to him. 'I'm afraid of highwaymen.'

Then when we were all standing in a line facing the hedgerow, watching Mr Millichip alight some distance away to perform his own necessities—for you can always depend on a valet for that—I said, 'Quick now, Jagger. What have you gleaned?'

'No more except that Gedge hates the sight of him from his heels to the top of his hat,' Jagger replied. 'Though can't say why in particular. He's been with Mr Dashwood eight or ten months now, and Gedge says a proper arse creeper. But for the rest, it seems he just come out into the mews as they was harnessing the hosses and announces, "Mr Dashwood's orders, and I'm to come with you". Gedge can't hardly deny him, and he don't say no more than that.'

'He's a rum un,' Maggsy broke in. 'I been sitting and keeping my mouth shut but watching him, and he never got that sunburn on his clock from brushing pantaloons and polishing boots. I reckon he looks more like a sporting cove. And, if he is, he's pretty sure to be a villain. That's where you've most likely seen him before,' the impudent wretch advised me. 'At one of these low-down race meetings or boxing matches you're always going off to when you get the chance.'

'It's not impossible,' I mused, thinking of sporting gentlemen and contemplating a fresh thought, then continuing, 'Now here's your instructions, Maggsy, when we get to the Plough at Brentwood,' and telling the little monster what I wanted him to do. 'A simple matter,' I concluded, 'if you're careful about it; and it might prove a pretty notion I have. So let's get back to the coach; and for a man who's lost his Pretty Polly, and don't know where to find her,' I added to Jagger, 'you look uncommon pleased with yourself.'

'No reason why not,' the cheerful fellow announced. 'I likes a jaunt like this, and I guessed the trollop was up to mischief from the start. I've no doubt we shall find her all right, and when we do I mean to up with her petticoats over her head, down with her pantaloons about her ankles, and slap her arse. There's nothing like that for coming to an understanding with a young lady, and I mean to come to mine with Miss Polly Andrews.'

'Well, I wish you joy of it, my lad,' I said, hiding my own forebodings as we turned back to the coach, on which Gedge had now got all his lamps flaring like beacons.

'And needs must,' the irascible old fellow growled as another curricle and a string of horses came rattling and clattering past to vanish into the darkness. 'I'd have her lit up like a gin parlour if I could, with all of these Bedlamite buggers loose on the road tonight.'

Mr Millichip was so far proved right, for as we passed the George at Brentwood the forecourt there was chock-a-block with lanterns, vehicles and travellers, all clamouring for cattle, whereas when we turned a bit off the main road to the Plough the stableyard here was dark and empty although the inn itself was still open and bustling. It was a simple matter to arrange our subterfuge. Mr Millichip got out of the coach and vanished into the shadows almost before we stopped, and the instant later Maggsy followed him, as silent as a cat and pretty near as invisible. When they had gone, one after t'other, I alighted myself, waited for Gedge to climb down, which he did with his back to the yard, and then said, 'Come now, Mr Gedge, we'll see what the supper-room has to offer. We can see about the horses after.'

'I keep telling you, there ain't going to be no hosses,' the bad-tempered old hunks replied frettishly, but he let me and Jagger steer him into the house without looking round too much, and once we had got him wedged into the crowd in the tap—all of 'em bawling their heads off about Boney's latest advance, for what little these simple yokels knew of it—the rest was easy.

Little more than a minute later Maggsy reappeared, giving me the thumb with his face alight with mischief, and when he had worked through to me he hissed in my ear, 'Just like you said. God's tripes, how did you work it out? I reckon somebody must've told you. I get myself behind a bale of hay, Millichip not seeing me, and he gives a whistle and the ostler comes from one of the stalls, and Millichip says, "We're all in the dumps", and the ostler says, "You're all cracked, but di'monds is trumps, and they're ready and waiting for you." And then something changes hands and the ostler says, "Thank you kindly," and I get out of it quick, and Millichip's close behind.'

That also was true enough, for, as Maggsy edged away, now with his look of angelic innocence, Mr Millichip next appeared at the door. This time I elbowed my way through the press to him, and he then murmured, 'It is all arranged, sir; the horses are being put in now. A mere mention of my Lord Bettsford. But if I might suggest, sir, it would look as well for Mr Gedge if you went out to the yard yourself.'

'I will,' I promised. 'On the instant. You're a tower of strength to us, Mr Millichip,' I said, 'as well as a mine of information. I see now that Mr Dashwood sent you with us for your special knowledge and influence.'

'I hope so indeed, sir,' he replied. 'I should much like to think so.'

We had lost half an hour, but not without a profit, and I had hopes of making it up by my next stratagem; namely, getting Jagger up on the box for a bit of hard driving. Neither was this all that difficult, for these coachmen are prodigious drinkers and pissers, although Gedge proved to be unexpectedly abstemious; perhaps from belonging to such a respectable household. Nevertheless, by the time we had consumed a quick supper—little more than a light snack of game pie, Melton pie, cold roast duck and various other assortments—I had contrived to get him outside a quart of strong ale, the same of claret and four or five glasses of brandy. So when we went out to the yard again he was pitching nicely in a strong cross sea with all sails set, and I said, 'You're tired, Mr Gedge, and no wonder. You'd best ride inside with us.'

'Thas right,' he mumbled. 'Hookham Priors las' night an' now Harrish, smore'n good hoss flesh c'n stand. That blurry ole fool Sloc'mbe.' Mr Millichip was viewing the scene with some disapproval, but he walked quietly round to the other side of the coach to get in and Gedge peered after him like a fuddled owl and then put his finger across his lips. 'Don' you lerron to him,' he whispered hoarsely. 'He's a shnake. But I'll tell you, Mr Sturrock. Shay they're goin' to assassicate Boney. But don' you believe it. Thas all gammon. He'sh goin' t'asasshinate Wellington. There must've been somethin' damnation wrong with that game pie,' he observed clearly and severely and then bellowed, 'B'nobody else is

goin' to drive my kerridge,' making a clutch at the steps up
to the box.

As might be expected, Jagger and Maggsy were half
killing themselves with laughing, but they were both still
quick enough. Maggsy had the door open, and Jagger said,
'No, you ain't uncle; in you gets now like a good daddy,'
heaved him from the back like a sack of oats, leapt for the
box, gathered up the ribbons, and bawled to the stable-lad
to let the horses go pretty well before me and Maggsy could
bundle in ourselves.

The rascal wheeled his leaders out with a rattle of hoofs, a
yell from the stable-boy, and a shower of sparks which might
well have been a foretaste of what was to come, damned near
tipping us over to start with. We was all in a heap except Mr
Millichip, who was still viewing the spectacle with disfavour, and by the time we had picked ourselves up and
shoved Gedge back into the corner of the opposite seat
Jagger was already clipping along at a smart pace.

After that, however, all might have been well but for the
carriage lamp which was lit inside, and had not Jagger
wheeled another corner too sharp to get out on to the
Colchester road. Gedge had now cursed himself breathless
and was making loud puffing noises like the fabled whale or
grampus, but the sudden lurch threw us all on our elbows
once more and roused him afresh, while a brighter flicker of
the lamp illuminated Mr Millichip for an instant. 'The devil
will have us all over before he's done,' Gedge announced,
and then seemed to perceive the unfortunate valet with
consternation and rage, crying. 'He's here again. What's he
doin' here? Thought we'd left him behind. I told you, he's a
snake. And what is worse than a snake in the grass?' he
demanded, fixing Maggsy with an uncertain eye.

'I dunno,' Maggsy replied, much enjoying himself. 'What about a porcuspine?'

'And you're a little rascal,' the cantankerous old fool announced. 'And Alfred the gardeners' boy is another. You ask Alfred,' he advised me cunningly.

'I'm game, then,' Maggsy answered, egging him on. 'Arshk Alfred what?'

'For God's sake, be quiet and let him rest,' I told the little wretch sharply, although I was starting to become more alarmed about our safety than Gedge's drunken ravings, for the coach was rocking in a most alarming manner, and Jagger was singing; which is always a bad sign with that reckless young devil.

He broke off to roar, 'R . . . o . . . ad there; give way!' and as we thundered past a covered wagon and a chorus of startled curses, Gedge observed, 'The devil is going too fast; it's a heavy coach this,' and then bellowed, 'Don't you tell me be quiet, Miss'turrock. It's my coach you're in. All I'm saying is you ask Alfred. You ask Alfred what he sees when he goes to the Hog in the Pound to put sixpence on an horse for McKechnie the gardener. Puts a shilling on for me as well sometimes,' he confided. 'But you ask Alfred when he sees that snake laughing and talking to Bully Wheeler there as thick as thieves.'

The mention of the Hog in the Pound caught my attention but, be damned, so did Jagger, the scoundrel. As every reader who has ever held the ribbons of a four-in-hand will know, there comes a point when a well-balanced coach will roll of its own weight, thus giving the horses little to do save keep pace ahead of it; but let that point be passed, as may be on a downward slope, and the coach begins to overrun the cattle to the most direful destruction of all, and then all you can do is to put your brakes on and address yourself to your Maker. It seemed to me that we were already well past that point and I had scant patience for either Mr Millichip or Gedge, but Millichip was plain losing his calm regardless of our danger, and he enquired, 'Mr Sturrock, are we to endure much of this?'

Gedge paused to bellow, 'Hold the horses you rascal,' and then jabbed an unsteady finger at Mr Millichip, while we all bounced about like peas in a colander, and continued, 'Endure as much as you like. *I* don't mind. All I'm saying is that the respectable are not Hog in the Pound . . . No; I got that wrong. The Hog in the Pound isn't respectable, nor is Bully Wheeler, and respectable persons shouldn't be seen there. Gardener's boys are diff'rent. Shee what I mean?' he asked me. 'He's a snake,' he cried. 'And I'm going to punch his nose.'

He lurched over to Mr Millichip as I shoved my head out of the window, and damned near got it lopped by something which came racing past the other way. Mr Millichip rapped out a most startling remark for a valet, Maggsy screeched, 'Whoa there, you old fool,' while I roared up to Jagger, 'Put your brakes on, you madman; you're overrunning!'

On that the coach started swaying like a cradle with the cavorting of the drunken lunatic behind me, him hiccupping that he'd flatten the shnake's nose, Maggsy screeching at him to hold off and hooting with horrid laughter, and Jagger bawling back from the box, 'What the hell are you doing in there? You'll have us over in a minute. I've just got the hosses nice in step.'

'I'll get you in step, you bloody maniac,' I yelled over the witch's bedlam, a further screech from Maggsy, a fresh bellow from Gedge, another word from Mr Millichip, then a sudden soft, sharp crack with Maggsy now crying, 'Jeeesus!' and something reeling into my back which very near had me out of the window. 'I'll have your liver out for this, Jagger,' I yelled afresh. 'Slow 'em down, I say. Stop 'em altogether.'

'Damned if I know what you're doing in there,' he complained, but started to screw the brakes down, and with heartfelt thankfulness I heard them begin to squeal on our rims and the fearful clatter of our cattle fall to a steadier pace. Only then, after offering up a further short prayer, did I draw my head back in; now to behold a spectacle of strange and singular peace. Mr Gedge lying back in his own corner, sleeping like a babe and a look of most melodious content on his face; Mr Millichip quietly smoothing the nap of his beaver with an expression as calm as a chamber pot; Master Maggsy regarding him in undisguised astonishment and admiration and a mouth as wide open as a parish oven.

'A most unseemly occurrence,' I observed in the silence. 'And might have upset us.'

I suspected that Mr Millichip more than half expected me to say something more or ask a question or two, but if he did he was mistaken, and after a further pause he also observed. 'A little too much drink taken, I would say.'

'That must have been the cause,' I agreed politely. And then added. 'I hope you haven't killed him. Lady Dorothea would be displeased.'

'Why, no,' he replied. 'I can assure you, sir. Just a gentle little tap. But I fancy it will keep him quiet for a time. And might I enquire why we are stopping?'

'I wish to remonstrate with my driver,' I said, as Jagger's somewhat aggrieved face appeared at the window. 'That lot was a bit too tasty.'

'Fine, spirited driving,' Mr Millichip cut in. 'If you'll

pardon me so rudely interrupting, sir. My late master, Lord Bettsford, would have praised it highly. My lord was a spirited whip with a four-in-hand himself.'

'Was he indeed?' I enquired. 'Well, don't let me go against anything my lord would have approved of. But don't you take that too freely either, you damned scoundrel,' I advised the now grinning Jagger.

'And another favour if I might ask it, sir,' Mr Millichip continued. 'Might it be permissible for me to ride with Mr Jagger?' He looked at our Sleeping Beauty. 'More convenient perhaps if Mr Gedge should awaken and feel inclined to continue the discussion.'

'A most commodious suggestion,' I agreed, thinking that it would give my good Jagger plenty of time for talk. 'And the air in here does stink like the inside of a brandy barrel.' But, according to the rhyming doggerel, there were two more stages to stop at yet, and Jagger had pulled in the coach with our lamps shining on a signpost which said 'Chelmsford IV miles'. There was no harm in encouraging Mr Millichip, and making my own plans easier to plot, and I continued, 'I'm fretted about our cattle, though. Jagger'll drive 'em to their knees before he's done. Do you have any further thoughts on where we might change 'em?'

He fell into it as neat as a whistle, affecting to ponder for a minute, then saying. 'Not Chelmsford, sir; that's certain. I doubt if there's a fresh horse in the entire town. We shall do better at a small place called Hatfield Peverel. And after that I'd suggest Marks Tey, just short of Colchester, which is close by my Lord Bettsford's seat. He is particularly well known there. And from Marks Tay to Harwich should be an easy stage.'

I suspected that Mr Millichip was enjoying himself, but

what he did not suspect was that so was I, for I said warmly,
'Mr Millichip, I don't know what we should have done
without you and my Lord Bettsford tonight.'

Fortunately, Master Maggsy chose to wait until he took
himself off to climb up to the box beside Jagger, but then
when we started to roll again the shrewd child enquired
sweetly. 'So who's gammoning which?'

'It's about half and half,' I replied. 'But I fancy Mr
Millichip might be going to have a small mishap soon. Our
only question is when. Whether at the next stage or a bit
later.'

'*Our* only question?' Maggsy repeated. 'Oh, no,' he said
hurriedly. 'You add me out. I don't aim to go mixing
nothing with that cove. He's dangerous. Godstrewth, I
never see anything like the way he give Gedge his quietus.
He fetched a right hand hook up so quick I never even see it
myself. And I didn't much like the look on his clock when the
old fool was dottering on about the Hog in the Pound
neither. He's the rummiest valet I ever seen.'

'Certainly a sporting gentleman if he's thick with Bully
Wheeler,' I agreed. 'There's food for thought in the connec-
tion between certain of Lady Dorothea's household and the
Hog in the Pound; which is why you'll do as you're told,
Master Maggsy. But we'll leave it until the last stage. I fancy
we might find some sort of message left there.'

'I don't like it,' the obstinate wretch persisted. 'If he's
going to assassingate Wellington he wouldn't think nothing
of knocking me off for starters.'

'He's not going to assassinate Wellington, you blockhead,' I said, though I must confess that it was a dreadful
thought, and an act not impossible in the heat of battle.
'That's no more than servants' hall gossip,' I added, hoping

to God it was.

'You don't want to be too sure,' he answered darkly. 'A right Johnny Simple you'd look if you let it happen. They'd put you out to grass for that all right. Suppose there's a secret hidden meaning in that rhyme? Something you haven't rumbled?'

'Maggsy,' I begged him, 'will you be quiet for a bit. For what it's worth I'll explain the rhyme to you. There is no meaning in it save the way it's written. "We're all in the dumps". One stroke. "For diamonds are trumps". Two strokes. "The kittens are gone to St Paul's." One stroke. "The babies are bit". Two strokes again. "The Moon's in a fit". One stroke. "And the houses are built without walls". The last two strokes. It's merely password and countersign for three staging-posts; so the ostlers shall recognise who the horses are bespoke for. And very likely pass on any messages that have been left.'

Maggsy grunted sceptically. 'It sounds like a lot of old taters to me.'

'It is,' I said, 'There was never any need of it. It's a fantastical notion thought of by a fantastical, romantic little fool. And I'd lay a wager that she's practised some such nonsense before with this young man Tom Debenham. It's what put the idea into her head. But that's all there is about the rhyme. The only thing that counts is where and how I found it.'

'In the waiting-room,' he recited, 'folded in *The Times* newspaper alongside the corpuss. So whoever corpussed him snitched whatever it was he was writing but never found the rhyme. But this cove Millichip knows all about it. It don't make sense.'

'No more it don't,' I said. 'That's what's important about

it. When your facts don't make sense there's a fair chance you're looking at 'em the wrong way round. Now, for God's sake, go to sleep, or sit quiet and think about it.'

Suiting the action to the word I affected to be dozing myself when Jagger pulled the coach to a stop some time later, while Mr Gedge was now snoring lustily, still oblivious to all things. Our carriage clock said half after one, and we were outside what seemed to be a smallish inn, dark and shuttered up but with a light burning in the outbuildings. Mr Millichip got down, saying, 'I'll see to it, Mr Jagger; but if you'll start loosing the traces we shall be off again quicker,' and on that Maggsy slipped out of the door on the other side. Then Jagger came to my side and I said very soft, 'That's right, my lad. Let him do it his own way. What do you make of him?'

'A pretty fair sort, I reckon,' Jagger replied. 'Leastways he's good company. Seems his last master was a sporting gentleman and he travelled a lot with him. But he's better content at Hanover Square as Mr Dashwood's more reliable with his wages, and he'd do anything to serve her ladyship.'

'And he might even be telling the truth. It's not unknown sometimes,' I mused, watching the light broaden out as a stable half door opened, seeing Mr Millichip framed in it with another fellow inside.

There was no sign of Maggsy in the dark, but after a very little while he eeled back into the coach observing softly, 'Right again. Every one a coconut. He says, "The kittens are gone to St Paul's", and the other cove answered, "You've kept me waiting up bleedin' late for it, but the moon's in a fit, and the hosses are ready for you." Then there was a bit more colloguing which I didn't catch, as the ostler reaches for a lantern and it looks as if he might spot me, so I shifted myself quick.'

'Just as well,' I told him benevolently. 'We don't want Mr Millichip to fancy we're prying. And now we're both wrapped in slumber if anybody should wish to know.'

So reclining in my corner with my beaver over my eyes I listened to the fresh team being brought out and put into the traces, a murmur of conversation and a laugh or two, and then Jagger's footsteps coming up to the window. The good fellow took the hint, for he said, 'They're all three asleep; we'll not disturb 'em,' after that there was the swaying of the coach as he and Millichip climbed up to the box, and in another minute more we were on the road again.

There seemed to be less traffic abroad now, or we were keeping up with it better, and Marks Tey turned out to be near enough two hours further; much of it taken up in trying to doze amidst the melody of Messrs Gedge and Maggsy's snores, and the rest in reflection. In short, whether what I might gain by incapacitating Mr Millichip for a short time would be worth the loss of trust and mutual esteem if he rumbled it. It would be easy enough to contrive a slight accident for him, but in the end I concluded that it would be best to let him go on being useful to us rather than risk turning him ill-tempered or frightening him off. Consequently, when Jagger pulled in for this stop, I did not even send Maggsy after him, but only alighted myself as if to stretch my legs and attend to other necessities.

The first dim light of summer dawn revealed a straggling village and another smallish inn, already stirring, for there was a wisp of smoke from the chimney and a fellow appearing in the yard at the sound of our arrival. In the uncertain gloaming it was hard to tell whether he and Mr Millichip were known to each other, but they stood in talk for a minute before both going into the stable, while Jagger busied himself about loosing the traces again. He gave me a grin over his shoulder, saying softly, 'He don't give much away. The only thing he owns to is liking to have a bit on the hosses, which he keeps dark from Mr Dashwood. But there ain't no harm in that, is there?'

It struck me that he was taking longer about the business here than at our two previous stops, but he seemed in no hurry when he appeared again, consulting his watch as he approached, and announcing, 'They'll be out directly, sir. We're doing very well. Once through Colchester it's a quick stage, and we should be at Harwich harbour before seven. I made so bold as to make certain inquiries here. They tell me that the Ostend packet sails at eight o'clock today, and a party meaning to go aboard her would most likely lodge at the Sloop Inn overnight.' He paused on that, and then continued, 'Mr Sturrock, it's not my place to pry into Family matters, but I hear there is some rumour of a plot to assassinate Bonaparte. Might I ask if that is correct?'

'Well now,' I replied, 'if it were I don't see why we should interfere. All the same I shall be thankful to catch that packet before she sails.'

'Indeed, sir, yes,' he agreed hurriedly. 'And I'm wasting valuable time in pointless talk. I ask your pardon.'

So we rolled on again, rattling through the still sleeping Colchester half an hour later, and after that nothing much more to report until Mr Gedge chose to wake himself, me and Maggsy with a thunderous fart and then a most prodigious belch. My first thought was that Jagger had overturned the coach, and Maggsy yelped. 'God help us, the battle's started; that's the cannons banging off,' while Gedge regarded us with a somewhat bleary gaze before coming down to earth and demanding, 'Who's driving?'

'Jagger,' I told him. 'You were a trifle indisposed after a game pie past its first freshness.'

'My oath it was,' he grunted. 'And must have been damnation tough as well,' he added, feeling his jaw tenderly.

'Do not discompose yourself, Mr Gedge,' I advised him, thanking God that he appeared to have forgotten Mr Millichip and the events of last night. 'We're doing very well. We're coming near to Harwich now.'

He grunted again, seeming to listen to the beat of our hoofs for a time, and then of a sudden looking as near amiable as he ever could. 'You need to be bloody near to it to get there with them hosses,' he announced. 'The inside leader's running dip-footed.'

To begin with I thought the old fool was merely cheering us on our way after his own coachman-like fashion, but little more than a minute later Jagger let out a sharp oath; and, when I thrust my head from the window to enquire what in damnation was the matter with them now, Mr Millichip replied, 'I fear, sir, that one of our leaders has cast a shoe.'

I shall add little more of that mishap, or of my own reflections that I should have done better to arrange an accident for Mr Millichip after all; of our limping pace for very near five miles to find a blacksmith, of our entreaties, threats and bribery before we could persuade the surly rogue to come from his bed and light his fire. These rude mechanics are much of a sort with coachman and hackney driver, and this one further professed never to have heard of Bow Street, and proposed that my Lord Bettsford should do something with himself which no gentleman would even consider, even were it possible. It is enough to say that we reached Harwich just in time to see the packet clearing the harbour with all sail set.

Six

Fortunately I am a man of patient, even mild disposition otherwise there might have been murder done. So there was nothing for it but to console ourselves as best we might with breakfast at the Sloop Inn, where several fine large fresh plaice and a pound of rare done steak apiece did something to restore us. Over this light repast Mr Millichip seemed somewhat chastened, as if he feared that I might blame him for the calamity, but I assured him kindly that anybody might lose a shoe—just as easy as anybody might loosen one in a stable, I added to myself—though, when he proposed that he should go to seek a fisherman or smuggler who might put us across, I sent Jagger with him in case he should next discover a boat with a hole in its bottom.

Then with Gedge announcing that he meant to sleep at the inn for the rest of the day and tonight, before returning peaceably to London tomorrow, Maggsy and I were left to our own devices. So thanking God to be shot of him as well I went on to our further inquiries, which proved to be unexpectedly easy, for the inn was quiet now and the landlord a talkative fellow with a sharp pair of eyes in his head.

A fairish party arrived about nine last night, he told us. A captain of the Tenth Dragoons, two grooms and a string of four horses, and two other young gentlemen also in military uniform but riding in a hired chaise. He noted them particularly as the house was uncommon crowded and the captain elected to sleep on the floor of the common room, leaving the last free private chamber to the other gentlemen. 'Proper well formed, they was,' he added, tipping me a wink. 'I knows two pairs of tits when I see 'em, however buttoned up they may be.'

With that we had to be content, but as we turned out of the inn to survey the harbour I said, 'So at least we know they got this far. And for want of half an hour we might have had 'em and saved everybody a lot of trouble. As it is now, God only knows what the end will be.'

' "For the want of a nail",' Maggsy quoted with one of his dazzling flights into poesy. ' "For the want of a nail a shoe was lost, for the want of a shoe a horse was lost, for the want of a horse a rider was lost, for the want of a rider a message was lost, for the want of a message a battle was lost . . ." I forget how it goes on,' he added hurriedly, seeing the look in my eye. 'But what I want to know is did Millichip do it? I asked Jagger, and he says it'd been easy enough, in the stable, and ostlers have been known to do it before now, specially with sporting events, but he swears Millichip never did. He says his language was very near as bad as yours when it happened, something horrible for a valet.'

I did not answer, for I was struck suddenly transfixed in the midst of the busy scene. The harbour alive with barges and ferry boats, two frigates putting out, several transports still being loaded, the wharf a confusion of cattle, men, supplies and even belated artillery. And in the midst of all, calmly surveying it, was the last figure I expected to see. 'Dear God Almighty!' I ejaculated.

'No, it ain't,' Maggsy said argumentatively, 'it's Major Finchingfield.'

As indeed it was, and I was off like a charge from a gun, damned near trampled underfoot by a string of kicking horses, just as close to getting brained by a net of round shot swinging overhead, falling foul of a squad of cursing artillery-men man handling a cannon, and plunging through a platoon of infantry. I had no need to attract the major's attention, for he heard the various observations before I reached him and turned to perceive me. 'Well I'm damned,' he said, 'Mr Sturrock. What're you doing here?'

It was on the tip of my tongue to tell him, and in no uncertain manner, but with my ever-present quickness it struck me that if he was truly what he seemed to be he might yet be of assistance. Putting on the manner of a poor flustered civilian I said, 'On Lady Dorothea Hookham's business, if you can spare a minute to hear of it. And if we can get out of this damned confusion for a bit.'

'It'll have to be quick,' he answered, nevertheless drawing me aside to a quieter place under a shed, where, still more flustered, I poured out our woeful tale, or as much as I thought good for him to hear. There wasn't much of it, and he listened in silence until I had finished and then observed, 'An elopement ain't army business, is it? All the same I'd like to help Lady Dorothea if I can.' He stood for a minute studying the transports, musing, 'It shouldn't be beyond me. Well enough,' he announced, 'I'll get you aboard the *Esmeralda*. She sails at noon, and she'll very likely be the last one. We're rushing this stuff over in the hope of stopping a few gaps.'

'What is the latest news?' I enquired humbly.

'Damned bad,' he said. 'The battle's imminent. Boney's

got every man, boy, horse and cannon he can lay his hands on, and he means to break through. And there are those who don't think we have a chance of stopping him.' With which encouraging information he finished, 'I must get back,' and moved away, only pausing to call over his shoulder, 'See you're here on time. We shan't wait for you.'

Even Maggsy was unwontedly sober. 'So we're going?' he asked.

'We're going,' I said. 'God help us. And I'll have some-body's guts out for this lot before I've finished with 'em.'

There is little to say of the interminable voyage. Having advised Gedge of our movements so that he could inform Lady Dorothea, procured a hamper of liquor and victuals from the Sloop Inn—I must confess on Mr Millichip's sage counsel—and left further instructions there and at the harbour master's office for my hoped for messenger from Burchall, we presented ourselves at the *Esmeralda* where Major Finchingfield was already waiting with some impatience. At first sight the guard at the gangway seemed inclinded to halt us, but the major announced briskly, 'Government courier and staff,' and a minute later we were aboard amid a fresh confusion of men, horses, supplies, artillery and ill-tempered sailors. 'You're not like to be noted much in this lot,' the major said, 'but you'd best keep out of sight. Find yourself a place for'ard in the bows. I'll come for a word with you when I may.'

Thereafter we passed a most uneasy but tedious day, and for my part I slept most of it, only roused at last by Maggsy plucking at my shoulder and muttering that the major was coming. It was then very dark, past two in the morning, the ship rolling and creaking uneasily with a long string of lights on our port side, and he was approaching carrying a lantern and picking his way over and around the sleeping figures on the deck. 'It's devilish slow,' he said. 'We're hove to, and going in at first light, for the harbour's crowded with shipping. But you should be ashore in a couple of hours or so.' He drew me aside to the rail, where he leaned a minute in silence, gazing across the water, before asking softly, 'Who's that other fellow with you?'

'Millichip,' I told him. 'Mr Dashwood's valet. Sent in case he might assist us. As he has; most providently.'

The he asked, 'Are you here only on a matter of this young fool eloping?'

'It's a matter of some importance to the family,' I replied.

He pondered on this for another minute, now watching a pinnace tacking out to the transport with hail and answer shouted to and fro. Then he continued, 'I played one or two slim tricks with you the other day, Mr Sturrock; though so did you with me. We're both men who hold our cards close. But I was damned perturbed when you seemed to take that murder for suicide. I'll be plain with you; I thought "This fellow's simple, and the less he's told the better".'

'Not so simple as I may seem,' I retorted, resisting an urgent desire to toss him overboard. 'You may be sure the murder is being fully investigated. It is not a practice we encourage at Bow Street. Nor is body-snatching. And now pray be good enough to tell *me* something, sir. What was your business with Lady Dorothea, and was it official or otherwise?'

'Unofficial,' he said. 'Mere goodwill. Fénelon had often spoken of her, and I meant to warn the lady against having any part in a damned dangerous plot he was hatching. But as things fell out I did not get the chance.'

'You're sure of that?' I demanded sharpish. 'That it was Fénelon's plot?'

'For God's sake,' the major cried impatiently, 'of course it was his plot. He's been on about it for weeks past. That's why they wouldn't touch him at the Horse Guards. God knows what would become of war if we took to assassinating each other's principals. But d'you see what it means? You have Fénelon planning to assassinate Boney with private assistance, and you have Fénelon murdered. It can only mean there's a Bonapartist agent or sympathiser in or close to Lady Dorothea's household. There are plenty of 'em about.'

'I see several things,' I said.

'I wonder if you do?' he enquired with an engaging manner which came near enough to giving me a stroke, 'D'you recollect that Lady Dorothea's husband, Mr Dashwood, is a Whig; and that when Boney got to Paris in March the Whigs was all for making peace with him? And d'you see that if he breaks through now he'll get his peace on his own terms. And then if he gets half a hint of any such plot against him at any time he'll demand a wicked revenge?'

The major was about to add something more, but on that instant there was a sudden command from somewhere aft, whistles blowing, sailors racing to the tackles and stumbling over the sleeping soldiers, and he cried, 'Begod, we're going in after all. That can only mean there's fresh news, and it's worse still. There's little more I can do for you, Mr Sturrock,' he continued hurriedly. 'I must be about my own business. But I'd say don't waste time searching for your party in Ostend. They must have landed here last night, and if they're travelling with ffoulkes he'll have had his orders to post to Brussels as quick as he could. I shall be posting on fast myself. I'd advise you to put up at the Reine de Suède in the rue de l'Évêque. It's good lodging, and if I hear of your people or ffoulkes I'll somehow contrive to get word to you there.'

Those last words were flung back over his shoulder as he hastened away into the throng of infantrymen, now rising from their slumbers and looking to their muskets and other gear, and as he vanished amid them Master Maggsy arose also from the shadow of the bulwarks, where he had been quietly listening to our enlightening conversation. 'What d'you make of that now?' he enquired. 'He tells a good tale, don't he?'

'A damned good tale,' I agreed. 'If you like that sort.'

This was the early morning of Thursday, June 15, near enough four o'clock before we finally got ashore amid a fresh urgency of shouted commands, men falling into rank on the quayside, kicking and squealing horses brought off, cannon and round shot swung out. Nevertheless, the port was already well awake and ablaze with lanterns and torches, and concluding that two hours or so at this juncture was neither here nor there we turned to the most commodious inn—or *hôtel* as they call them in these parts—where we refreshed and cleansed ourselves of the stains of travel; and where I discovered with interest that Mr Millichip spoke French very near as good or perhaps even a trifle better than my own. We saw no further sign of Major Finchingfield, but, despite his opinion and the bustle all around us, I made my own inquiries, with the result much as he had foretold; namely, that a party such as I described had supped hurriedly the night before and then left at once for Brussels, but now having another gentleman riding with them.

With that much clear, and after leaving further messages for Burchall's courier, we set off ourselves about seven; on which journey there is again little to describe. Save for two pretty little towns, where the church bells were ringing the alarm, the country is featureless; the peasants suspicious and the post-house keepers surly and avaricious—though they brightened somewhat at the sight of good English sovereigns. It was sweltering hot and dusty throughout, and towards midday we heard the sound of heavy gunfire to the south; which continued on and off throughout the afternoon. Nevertheless we advanced resolutely and even made pretty good time, despite delays occasioned by marching columns, supply trains and artillery hastening on the capital against an increasing throng of carriages, wagons and people afoot hurrying fearfully the other way. It was a sure sign of the terror this damned Corsican madman inspired, and at the last post house we were refused fresh horses on the grounds that they would very likely be snatched from us as soon as we got to Brussels. There was a report that he had promised his troops six hours' sack of the city when they entered it; though Mr Millichip was of the opinion that this was a false rumour put about by his agents there to increase the alarm and confusion.

But it would have taken a desperate man to snatch horses from Jagger and we reached the rue de l'Évêque in good order by about six o'clock, still with the sound of gunfire hammering in the air and now seeming to be louder. The Hôtel la Reine de Suède proved to be a commodious establishment, where there were several English officers lodging, and a brief mention of the Duke of Richmond to the patron immediately secured us the best attention. Then once again removing the dust of travel I took out a fresh neckcloth and my best frockcoat and pantaloons—which Mr Millichip kindly offered to brush and press for me—and, thankful to be about some positive work once more, set out to find the Richmond residence in the rue de la Blanchisserie.

This was not all that far from the *hôtel*, and on presenting my letters to the footman I was not kept waiting above a quarter of an hour in the ante-room before a very pretty young lady appeared. Speaking somewhat breathlessly she said, 'Mr Sturrock? You are welcome sir; indeed any friend of Lady Dorothea's is very welcome, and what a foolish creature Georgina Wilde is, to be sure; though many like her have come out here to be near their dear ones. And I have given your other letters to my papa, and he asks me to assure you of his service, though you may understand that in our present distraction . . .'

She paused, and I replied, 'More than distractions, my lady,' giving my best bow. 'But my first request is the simplest. I need to find a certain Captain ffoulkes of the Tenth Hussars.'

'Captain ffoulkes?' she repeated. 'I do not know of him myself; there are so many officers. But he may be at our ball tonight; or perhaps some other who may know him.'

'A ball, my lady?' I asked, not a little surprised and reflecting on the sound of cannon, the people hurrying out of the city and all the other signs of approaching battle.

'It does seem strange, does it not,' she agreed. 'Mama asked the General if she should put it off, but he told her on no account.' Lady Georgiana lowered her voice. 'It's well known that Brussels is positively infested with Bonapartists, a half of the Belgians at the very least, even some of one's own servants; it will do no harm to let them see that we don't

care a fig for the Ogre. If it pleases you to attend, Mr
Sturrock, I'm sure that is the best way you may hear
something of your Captain ffoulkes.'

'I shall be most obliged and honoured to attend, my lady,'
I replied, bowing once more.

After some further politenesses on both sides I withdrew
and returned to the *hôtel*, at once gratified by the invitation
to such an elegant and defiant occasion, sanguine that I
might indeed discover something of Captain ffoulkes and
the two naughty young women, and perturbed that I had no
evening dress for the function. But here again our ever
resourceful Mr Millichip assured me that Lord Bettsford
had several times found himself in a similar predicament,
and, after consultation with the patron, produced a tailor
who professed himself perfectly able to fit me out with
something at least decently suitable; which he did well and
expeditiously, while I reflected that Lady Dorothea could
not but consider it a reasonable expense.

It is worth noting here that Master Maggsy was growing
increasingly jealous of Mr Millichip's ever-readiness, and
when we were alone in my chamber for a minute, considering the general effect and trying on the gloves for fit, he
observed darkly. 'That cove's on the gammon, and I dunno
what you're about neither. What d'you mean to do with
him?'

'Why,' I said, in great good humour, 'either see him
hanged in the end, or take him on as my own valet if he's not.
I ain't just sure which yet.'

Then after giving him, Jagger and Mr Millichip all
together their further instructions—that they were to quarter
the city in close company, and make their own inquiries as a
second string to our bow—I repaired to the dining-room,

where there were several of the officers already being served; and, by the splendour of their apparel, also bound for the Duchess of Richmond's ball. The cannonading had now stopped, leaving an oppressive silence after the rumbling and tremble in the air, and I made so bold as to enquire what the battle was and where it had been.

Considering I was a civilian they were pretty polite. They looked me up and down somewhat, but one of them vouchsafed, 'Boney's crossed the river Sambre and attacked the Prussians,' while for my further enlightenment another added, 'Made a surprise move and drove in von Zieten's corps. Gave 'em a damnable mauling.'

With that I had to be content, and expressing myself obliged I left them to their own low-voiced discussion.

But if the news was alarming there was little sign of it in the rue de la Blanchisserie, for the street was thronged with carriages and lamps and curious onlookers—some of 'em not all that amiable or well-wishing in the face, I noted— and the ballroom itself brilliant with uniforms and elegant gowns and beautiful women. Otherwise, however, I shall take it upon myself to set right a mistaken notion of it largely put about later by the poet, Lord Byron, who was not present; namely, that the function took place in a splendid mansion. To be precise the Richmonds' residence was quite modest for persons of their wealth and rank, being—as I learned afterwards from Lady Georgiana—the property of a coachmaker, from whom it was rented, while the ballroom had at one time served as a storehouse for his carriages, and was now commonly used as a playroom and schoolroom for Lady Georgiana's younger sisters. It was connected with the rest of the house by a further ante-room; and, so far from being all marble and chandeliers, it was decorated simply with a pretty but somewhat faded trellis and rose pattern wallpaper.

But it is the company which makes the occasion, not the surroundings, and here tonight you had everything from princes down to mere baronets and knights. In short, the *créme de la créme* of the nobility and military of Britain, Prussia and the Low Countries; and a spectacle, could they but have seen it, to give pause for reflection to Bonaparte and his raggle-taggle of butchers, bakers and candlestick makers.

None the less, it was a strange affair, for after I had paid my respects to my host and hostess—who greeted me kindly though it was plain to see that they had clean forgotten who I was—accepted a glass of champagne from a footman and moved aside to view the glittering scene, I noted that there were tears close under the laughter of many of the ladies, however they were romping in the polonaise and quadrille or swirling in the waltzes. It was to be observed also that, while the younger officers were dancing as gaily as if they were merely going shortly to a review rather than a deadly battle, their seniors were conversing together in close groups, and that from time to time dusty messengers hurried in to one or another of them. 'As good as a hunt ball, ain't it, Keppel?' I overheard one young dragoon cry, to which the second replied. 'Well, ain't that what it is, Charley? Ain't we going to hunt 'em tomorrow?'

I was so taken up by this spectacle and certain profound reflections that for a time I near enough forgot my prime purpose, and now recalling myself to my own simpler duty I set to scrutinising the brilliant throng, wondering if I did not discover Captain ffoulkes whether perhaps Major Finchingfield might appear, or even Miss Georgina herself; for this was the kind of affair which would attract her like a bee to honey. Needless to relate I observed no sign of any of them, but I was sharply reminded of the danger and suspicion abroad in Brussels that night as a voice behind me demanded, 'Are you seeking something, sir?'

I turned to behold a positive giant of a cavalryman, such a blaze of colour about his breeches and dolman and sabretache that he fairly dazzled the eye; and also more than a little inebriated, and agressive with it. 'Been watching you,' he informed me, viewing my hired dress coat with evident distaste. 'Fellow's got a damned Frenchified look about him,' he continued to his companions. 'Shall we have him out?'

'I'm as English as yourself, sir,' I retorted. 'But I am seeking someone. And if you can assist me, I shall be obliged. A Captain ffoulkes of the Tenth Hussars.'

If anything this seemed to incense him still more, for he observed, 'A damned tradesman, eh? A blasted tailor dunning a poor fellow for his bill, is it? Then let me tell you, my man; this ain't the time nor place for tradesmen.'

So enraged I was that there might well have been an unseemly incident at the ball, and spoiled my chances for good, had not one of the others cried, 'No, Jack, let the gentleman be. See, now, there's Molly Flinders waving to you,' and thus contriving to steer him away. But the one who had spoken turned back to add, 'If it's the Tenth you're looking for, I fancy they're already ordered out. Haven't a notion where, though. Nobody knows anything all that much.'

Reflecting that fine feathers don't of necessity make a peacock and that it might be wiser to continue my watch from some more secluded corner, I took shelter with a group of the few other civilians present. Indeed I was half minded to give the matter up, though reluctant, until I descried Lady Georgiana looking about, then catching my eye and beckoning to me with her fan. So now working my way around the edge of a thunderous cotillion I discovered her in conversation with one of the officers from the Hotel de Suède; and, still speaking a little breathless, she said, 'Mr Sturrock, this is Captain Verner of the Seventh Hussars, and he will help you if he can.' It turned out that he could add little to what I already knew; that he did not know ffoulkes himself and imagined he must be a new fellow, and when I enquired further about an ensign of the Fifty-Second Oxfordshire he said, 'Oh, that's worse still. That's like looking for a pebble on the seashore. But wait now,' he added, 'I'll see what I can find out about the Tenth.'

He turned away obligingly to engage a further officer and Lady Georgiana remarked, 'What a headstrong girl it must be. But it's quite romantic, Mr Sturrock. Is it so serious?'

'Ma'am,' I said, 'if all I see and suspect is correct it is very serious. It's urgent I find this young lady before worse befalls her.'

'It's so difficult,' Lady Georgiana sighed, 'in all this confusion. Who knows how many of these dear friends we shall ever see again when it's all done? And some of these girls so *heartless*.'

She was near enough in tears, though putting a brave front on it, and it was plain she regarded my inquiries as a trivial matter. I hardly knew what further to say to her, but on that Captain Verner returned, also seeming still more preoccupied, and said, 'The Tenth's in position. Astride the road by some place called Quatre Bras. And if your man arrived this morning . . .' he continued, but then broke off to announce, 'Hulloa; here's the Duke. Now we may hear something.'

I turned to see Wellington enter with some of his staff and the Duke of Richmond, in his sober blue frockcoat a plain figure amid all the other gaudy plumage, yet tall and commanding; grave and thoughtful, but composed. It was clear he wished his entrance to be unobstrusive, for he moved quietly aside to a sofa, where he sat conversing with several of the ladies. But from time to time he leaned back to give instructions to the gentlemen grouped behind, or exchanged a few words with one or another of the senior officers as they approached him and then just as unobtrusively left the ballroom. This was over the space of a number of cotillions, quadrilles and waltzes as the younger people still whirled gaily in a kaleidoscope of gowns and uniforms to the strains of music and laughter.

But it was clear that great events were portending, for next appeared another messenger accompanied by a still more magnificently attired officer, little more than a boy; and one of the ladies close by me whispered. 'The Prince of Orange; and *so* handsome.' The messenger now retired to an alcove, as if to await his further orders, while the Prince approached the Duke's sofa to lean over the back, hand him a note and whisper in his ear; to which the Duke nodded once or twice, though still with no change of countenance, and then rose with a bow to the ladies and a word to Richmond and his staff. This was not half a dozen paces from me and, as if talking of indifferent matters, they all passed by in no great hurry to the ante-room leading to the residence; and I shall confess that I was so bold as to follow them. It was forward, perhaps even discourteous, but few men are privileged to see the Muse of History unfolding her design and I was just in time to hear the Duke ask Richmond, 'Have you a good map in the house, Charles? Napoleon's humbugged me, by God; he's gained twenty-four hours on me,' while another officer called to an orderly, 'Webster! Four horses instantly to the Prince of Orange's carriage for Waterloo.'

It was a dramatic moment, but I felt it prudent to draw back to the ballroom; and just as well I did, for I now perceived that that damned Captain Bobadil of a cavalry-man had his eye on me again, and was even thrusting his way through to me. 'This,' I said to myself, 'may be damned awkward; I shall have trouble with this fellow before he's done,' but stood my ground, taking a further glass of champagne from a passing footman. Boldness is ever the best policy, and as he approached I enquired, 'Well, sir? What may I do for you now? If you wish to enquire of my credentials pray address yourself to his grace the Duke of Richmond; when he has time for you. But I may advise you that I am here on the business of my friend Lady Dorothea Hookham of Hanover Square.'

It produced a most astounding result. 'Dear Dottie Hookham?' he cried. 'F'God's sake why didn't you say so? Horse-faced,' he confided to his friends, 'An' a blue stock-ing, but the dearest, kindest woman in London; kindest woman in all England,' he added. 'Known her f'years. Knew her brother; was at Eton with him. Damn good fellow he was. Know her cousin, old Roddy Wilde-Hookham. Mad as a hatter.' He stopped suddenly, and then continued, 'Tell you what. Swear I saw the filly today.'

'The filly?' I repeated. 'Miss Georgina Wilde-Hookham?'

'S'right,' he said. 'Saw her plain as I see you.' I reflected briefly that there was some doubt whether he was capable of seeing me all that plain, but he continued, 'Two of 'em, getting out of a chaise. A brace of ensigns. Looked me straight in the eye, but thought nothing of it. Whoever does look at ensigns? B'then it struck me after. "By God, that was Georgie Wilde!" I says.'

'Where, sir?' I demanded urgently. 'Where?'

He paused on that, pondering heavily before confessing. 'Now there you have me. I'm damned if I can recollect. Got a head like a colander.'

You've got a head full of champagne, I thought, and as if to confound me still further supper was announced then, and he was carried off again by his companions and several young ladies who should have had more sense of a grave occasion. But I am not a man to let his quarry escape having got so close to it, and I followed hard on their heels to the supper-room, now noting that Wellington was seated between the Duchess of Richmond and Lady Georgiana Lennox, and conversing as amiably as if he had been in Belgrave Square. The Muse of History could do what she liked with her designs now, however, for I had other business on hand. I ran him down again in a fresh bevy of young ladies, to whom he appeared to be vastly diverting, and at risk of their displeasure drew him aside firmly saying, 'Sir; it is most urgent and important that I find Miss Georgina Wilde-Hookham. If I do not it might well cost the young lady her life.'

That seemed to sober him somewhat. 'What?' he demanded. 'You don't say she means to fight? I wouldn't count it past her. An' they say Boneys got women in his cavalry.'* He winked at me. 'Fine jape to capture one, eh?'

* This appears to have been correct. After the battle the body of one very beautiful young woman was found near Mont St Jean, at a point she could not have reached unless she was riding in one of the prodigal French cavalry charges during the afternoon of June 18.

'Let us not be frivolous, sir,' I admonished him sternly. 'Where did you see Miss Georgina?'

'Oh, be damned,' he replied, 'I've told you, I can't recollect. Lemme see now. Twasn't at Dalrymple's party last night. N'yet at whist after; wouldn't play with 'n ensign. 'Smornin' went riding out to clear my head; 's far as St Jean. Devilish lot of infantry there. Might've been at St Jean.'

'But was it?' I persisted. 'You said she was getting out of a chaise.'

'Now listen,' he said, beginning to turn dark in the face and clapping a heavy hand on my shoulder, 'let it be, there'sh a good fellow, or I shall get annoyed. I've got to make my adieux to these ladies.'

Though fretting with impatience I had to be content with that, for I could not treat him like a Bow Street case and it was clear that if I turned him ill-tempered again I should get little but an unseemly incident. All I could do was to keep close by him and pray that he might sober up a little before he was called away, how ever many black looks and unfavourable comments it might earn me. And thank God I did, for the end and enlightenment came suddenly, but not before close on three o'clock. There was a stir at the entrance doors and one more officer appeared, making a signal to silence the band and announcing. 'You gentlemen who have engaged partners had better finish your dance and muster as soon as you can.' (And this order, by the way, was how some officers came to fight the battles of the next three days still in their evening dress.)

Despite my now extreme disfavour I could not but ask who that was, and one of my man's companions replied shortly, 'Lord Uxbridge; commanding the cavalry,' and added, 'Come on now, Stanny. Steady yourself, you fool.

We're mustering in the Place Royale.'

On that a beaming smile overspread his face. 'Tha's it,' he cried. 'The Place Royale. Was riding through the Place Royale at eight this morning. And that's where I saw the filly. Gettin' out of a chaise.'

I barely paused to thank the gentleman, but hurried away to claim my beaver, gloves and cane, at the same time asking the footman, 'What hotels are there in the Place Royale, and how do I get there quickly?'

'The Hôtel Bellevue, monsieur,' the man answered. 'Your quickest route is to turn *à droite* for a short distance, then cross the street and pass through the park.'

In my haste and thankfulness I very nearly gave him a soverign, but thought better of it just in time.

In the city now all was martial, as in the ballroom it had all been laughter and music. It was the general order to arms; a bugle sounding the turn-out in the night some distance away, and another answering farther off still; the rumble of supply trains on the cobblestones; the skirl of bagpipes and tramp of marching feet, a drum and fife band striking up 'The British Grenadiers', another troop lustily singing 'The Girl I Left Behind Me'. I fell into the military quick march myself as I stepped down the street, thrusting through the idle bystanders—and more of 'em about than ever—and waiting impatiently for a string of carriages to come flying past before I could turn across into the quiet and darkness of the park.

I was not displeased, for I had pretty well bottomed the matter by now; and entirely from my own observation of all the events and parties concerned and all that had been said. Much must depend on Burchall's report confirming my

conclusions, and if the man travelled fast his courier should
arrive here not much after noon today; but I had long since
discarded the notion of a plot to assassinate Bonaparte—
indeed, I had done so since before leaving London; and even
if there had been any such plot I should not have considered
it my business to interfere, providing only Frenchies were
concerned in it—although I was still somewhat puzzled and
perturbed by Gedge's drunken observations during the
drive to Harwich.

These, I considered, merited at least a report to the
proper authorities if I could offer it without making myself
seem ridiculous; something which it seemed was all too easy
with these military gentlemen. Apart from this all that
remainded was to find these two foolish young women, warn
them of their danger and if necessary place them under
restraint, perhaps at the Duke of Richmond's residence,
until I could remove it. No doubt there would be some
uncommonly pretty fireworks flying when Miss Georgina
Wilde-Hookham and I spoke our minds to each other, but
the first essential was to have it all done quickly, before the
tide of battle rolled over us. I had considered that Wellington's demeanour, though resolute, was that of a man who
perceives the situation is far graver than he thinks it wise to
admit. In short, that Brussels was a very fine place to be out
of fast.

By now I could see and hear the Place Royale not far
before me, though still in the darkness of the park myself;
lanterns and torches moving, troops falling into rank, the
cavalry mustering, shouted commands and the beat of
drums. With all this, and deep in my own thoughts, I did not
note the several shadowy figures close behind. The first I
knew of the attack was an unknown voice muttering *'Vite'*,

and then they were on me.

Had I been armed with only one of my Wogdons the end would have been different, but a gentleman does not take pistols to a ball any more than the supposed Captain Fénelon took a pistol to Lady Dorothea's house. None the less I gave a pretty good account of myself. One rascal I laid low with a snouter, and must have pretty near taken the eye out of another with a slash of my cane. But in a brawl of this sort, as I have often advised the ladies, you are lost if you cannot get your back against a wall. There were four of 'em, and they meant to have the business done quick. My beaver was swept from my head and a cudgel—or it might have been a musket butt—descended; I perceived a coruscation of lightnings, and forthwith sank into repose.

Seven

I came to with all the hammers of hell beating on all the anvils within my head; and also seeming to slap at my ears until I came to perceive by slow degrees that this much at least was cannon fire again, for with each reverberation there was a little tinkle and rattle from somewhere close by. It was total darkness and I was half reclining against a wall, as if I had been flung down like a sack, while I at length concluded somewhat painfully by this said little tinkle and rattle and a certain vinous odour that I was in some kind of wine cellar; as I further concluded that I must have been here for some hours, since I had been struck down at a little past three o'clock in the morning, and the gunfire now sounded like a heavy engagement. In this I was correct, learning later that I had been listening to the twin battles of Ligny and Quatre Bras on Friday, 17 of June; the first when the Prussians under Blücher and Gneisenau were defeated and forced to withdraw, and the second when our own troops and the Netherlanders fell back towards Waterloo.

But I was presently more concerned with my own precarious situation than the outcome of battles, and not in the best of tempers, especially on finding a lump pretty well the size of a small cannonball itself on the side of my cranium. As I gathered my scattered wits I discovered uncertain recollections of having half awakened several times before, on one occasion when I fancied some rascal with a lantern had come in to peer at me; so now concluding that if he had come once he would come again, and resolving when he did to give him the sweetest surprise he had ever had in his life, I got myself on to my feet to grope about the confines of my prison like blind-man's buff.

It did not take long, for there was not much of it. Wine racks, but not all that big and not many bottles, rough walls, a heavy timber door, quite immovable; and about shoulder height an equally heavy wooden partition beyond which I fancied I could hear and smell horses. But when I went back to stand with my ear against the door I could hear no other sound. 'So we have a smallish cellar, half underground, and close by a stable,' I mused. 'So it might well be one of the lesser post houses, or one of the little inns these savages would call an *estaminet*. And they don't mean to kill me. Or not just yet. Very likely meaning first to discover how much I know about 'em and their plot. But, by God, they shall learn their mistake,' I said aloud. 'The man who puts Jeremy Sturrock to bed in a place where he may find both refreshment and armament is a fool. If they want rough fighting, they shall have it.'

With these observations I next groped about once more to light on the first bottle that came to hand, knock its neck off and take a deep though careful draught; when, much to my surprise, I found it was a fine, full Burgundy of excellent vintage. I shall confess that I might have done well to reflect more on this, but I was still somewhat ill-tempered and merely took up my position beside the door, listening to the cannon fire again, wondering what time of day it was, reflecting on the nature of my assailants, and speculating on what Master Maggsy and Jagger might be doing to find me. All being equally fruitless.

But I did not have long to wait. I had scarcely finished the first bottle, and reached out for a second, before I heard footsteps outside and a key grating in the lock, but no sound of voices. That was my further undoing; for as the door swung open in a glow of light and only one man appeared, holding his lantern up high to see the better, I crowned him clean and crisp. Then without waiting to study the rascal as he swayed on his feet, somewhat surprised, I flung him aside and stepped out into a passage. But there were three more of them there, two armed with cocked pistols, and all dressed in some sort of livery; at which a most horrible and confounding suspicion crossed my mind.

I am a brave man, sometimes even rash. I have been known to face one pistol—hoping to God it might misfire— but not two; and never when there is no way of escape behind me. None the less I put a bold face on it. 'Come now,' I demanded. 'What damned nonsense is this?'

'You'll find out soon enough,' one of them replied. 'We've orders to bring you easy if we can, but to shoot to disable if you turn awkward. And we shall. Make no mistake of it. So you'd best march quiet.'

'I'll be damned if I'll march,' I told him. 'Not until I know what you're about.'

The fellow ignored me, only saying, 'Jules, you best get in there to see what he's done to Antoine,' and then adding, 'Now march.'

There are times when a wise man withholds his defence and says no more. In short, I marched. Along this passage,

up a flight of stone steps to a better sort of corridor and into a
hall which I recognised with growing surprise and foreboding; past an ante-room beyond which I could see the trellis
and rose-sprigged wallpaper of last night's ballroom. For I
was in the residence of the Duke of Richmond.

The Duke received me, if that be the word, in his study. He
was seated behind his desk, before a window which was
rattling in the cannonade, a very different figure from the
genial host, and his first words were, 'Well, sirrah, what
have you to say for yourself?'

'Your grace,' I replied, as polite as I could, 'I might
answer that better if I knew how I came here and why. And
why I was incarcerated in a cellar.'

'You are here,' he said, regarding me with evident disfavour, 'because you were discovered in our carriage yard
this morning by my coachman. At first, it seems, he thought
you were drunk and then he took you for dead. But there
were certain papers half protruding from your coat pocket,
and these he proceeded to examine in the hope of dicovering
who you might be. I must warn you that I have those papers
before me now.'

'Come, my lord,' I protested, growing warmer as he got
colder, 'I'm damned certain I had no papers about me to
warrant this treatment. I am attacked in the park by four
unknown ruffians; though I fancy I could put names to the
party or parties who set 'em on to it. I wake to find myself
treated like . . .'

'You wake to find yourself treated as a Bonapartist spy
should be treated,' he interrupted. 'If indeed you're not
something worse; a would-be assassin. You present yourself

to us with forged credentials, you abuse our hospitality,* and it appears you are engaged about a most dastardly crime. I must advise you that I have informed the Provost Marshall's office. Fortunate for you they are busy about other matters presently, and I have been requested to keep you close until they have time for your case. And keep you close I shall. On the evidence I have here you will hang, Sturrock; if that is your name.'

My God, I *am* in a sweet pickle this time, thought I. But with what calm I could muster I said patiently, 'I am Jeremy Sturrock of the Bow Street police force, and I am here about my legal duties. To wit, the murder of a certain Frenchman masquerading as a captain of Bonaparte's Twelfth Chasseurs with intent to obtain money by false pretences from Lady Dorothea Hookham-Dashwood; the illicit removal of the said Frenchman's body from a public mortuary; and the intended abduction of a young lady of rank and wealth, the same being a close relative of Lady Dorothea.' This seemed to give his grace pause for a minute and, seizing my advantage, I enquired. 'Am I permitted to see this evidence against me?'

'I cannot refuse you that,' he admitted, and pushed one paper across the table to me as if he were afraid it might burn his fingers.

Not surprisingly it was that ranting proclamation which Maggsy had discovered in the Hanover Square carriage; and I now wished heartily that the mischievous little wretch

* Sturrock was not the only one. Unknown to the Duke of Richmond there actually was a French spy at the ball; one of Bonaparte's generals wearing a Belgian uniform. There were so many uniforms, many of them unrecognisable, that Richmond greeted this man warmly, shaking hands with him and saying, 'We shall have sharp work soon; I am glad to see you here.'

had left it there. But I said 'My lord, it is well known that this rubbish was published some weeks since in Paris. As you must be aware yourself we have our own agents there and several copies were sent to London. When, I may say, it caused considerable merriment at the Horse Guards. I'm told that the Prince Regent was particularly amused. This one was brought to my notice at Bow Street.'

It appeared that His Royal Highness was not among the duke's most favoured gentlemen, for he observed acidly. 'Let us hope that the Prince Regent's amusement was well founded; and that it extends itself to Brussels. And let us hope also that you can explain this so easily.'

So saying he thrust a second paper at me. And what with three nights pretty well without sleep, a bump on the head, and my present perplexities I damned nearly had an apoplexy when I took it in. It was in the form of a letter, it was in French, and it was more than enough to hang me. It said: 'M. Sturrock; you may be assured that your service will not pass unrewarded. We have certain information that W. will be present at Lady of Richmond's ball, where you may regard him. It is not expected that an attempt should be made here. In our advice the best and most natural will be in the field. The custom habitual of W. to ride freely about his army is well observed and such circumstance the Nassau regiments should be noted. A Nassau uniform or uniforms may be provided if you desire them. We repeat our assurances that your interest will not march unregarded, even to the Emperor.'

Seeing me struck speechless the Duke enquired, 'You've nothing to say, then? Pray tell me if you can, what manner of man is it who would even contemplate such a thing?'

'By God, I've plenty to say,' I retorted. 'What manner of

man is it who'd think this of me?' I tossed the paper back at him, saying, 'It's a palpable forgery. It wouldn't take in a child.' But then seeing by the look on his face that honest indignation would not get me far I continued more soberly, 'I've heard of these Nassauers. But who and what are they?'

'Contingents raised from the County of Nassau in Germany,' he replied. 'It's territory that's been under Bonaparte for some years past, and many of the men have served in his armies. They're known to be unreliable, and I myself consider it a mistake to employ them at all; but they're stiffened with British Officers, and we're so short of troops to fill the gaps . . .' He broke off hard on that, as displeased with himself as he was with me, and added, 'We're not here to discuss tactics.'

'No sir,' I agreed. 'But we're not here to condemn a man without a hearing either. Pray permit me to relate my side of it.' And before he could stop me I embarked on my tale, from the shot in Hanover Square and Major Finchingfield to Mr Millichip and the journey to Brussels and now my present predicament. 'So there we have it,' I concluded. 'Two very quick, clever rascals who take every chance that's offered them and make a trick with every card they play.'

As I finished that I had a sudden light of inspiration as to where I had seen Master Millichip before, but thought no more of it then, for his grace the Duke said, 'Excellent. A most excellent story if I were in a mood for entertainment. But I fear I'm not. If you are a Bow Street officer *par exemple* why have you not arrested these men?'

Steady, Sturrock, I admonished myself, keep your choler down, and continued reasonably, 'First, sir, until I receive messages from London, which I am expecting today, I have no proof. Second; short of Ensign Debenham or Captain ffoulkes—who by now will be on the battlefield—they might have led me to Miss Georgina Wilde-Hookham and her maid. I might add that I had high hopes of finding these two foolish young women myself at the Hotel Bellevue early this morning; which hopes are now dashed by my unjust imprisonment in your hospitable wine cellar. And third, because I have no legal standing or power of arrest here in Brussels. Indeed, I had also hoped to enlist your aid in that respect.'

The good gentleman stroked his chin, gazing at me thoughtfully for a minute before observing, 'You're not without impudence; and even courage of a sort. But you're a dangerous fellow, my man, and you must return to this hospitality of my wine cellar. I cannot have you in the house to the fright and offence of my wife and daughters. I'll see it's made a little more comfortable. You shall have food and a lamp brought in, and attend to your necessities under guard. But there you must stay until we've time to deal with you.'

He nodded to the two men who had brought me in, still standing behind me, and I thought swiftly that if honesty and fair words had failed all I had left now was my wits. I said, 'One moment, sir, if you please. My courier from London should be in Brussels by now, and his information might do much to corroborate my story. In common justice will you send to the Hotel de Suède instructing him to bring his messages here to you?'

His grace considered this for a minute and then nodded briefly, while I reflected that if the fellow had not yet arrived I could well be lost, though it would advise Jagger and Maggsy where I was and I might hope for something from that little monster's wicked cunning. I continued, 'And the matter of the young ladies, my lord. I doubt they are there

now; but if you will further enquire for Miss Georgina
Wilde-Hookham and her maid Polly Andrews at the Hotel
Bellevue it may also assist me.'

'Why the devil should I assist you?' he enquired.

'It's my neck in question,' I reminded him feelingly. 'And
there's one more thing yet. Will you send to the Quartermaster-General, Sir William de Lancey; to ask him whether
he had, or has ever had, a Major Finchingfield on his staff?'

But that was too much for the anxious gentleman. 'What
d'you suppose that is?' he demanded, waving his hand at the
rattling and shaking window. 'Don't you think Sir William
might have more to do than answer tomfool questions? Take
him away,' he said to the two men; and then, as a final
blessing, added, 'I'll give you fair warning, my good fellow.
If we have to fight for Brussels or evacuate I'll see you
hanged first as an example to all the other scoundrels of your
kidney about the place.'

Apart from that I was treated with every courtesy. A chair
and a lamp brought in, and a mattress put on the floor for
further luxury; it wanted only the Bible which they kindly
present to the condemned prisoners in Newgate for their last
night. But at least with the light I could see to choose which
vintage I fancied from the racks, and tell the time by my
watch; now discovering to my further consternation that it
was gone five o'clock in the afternoon.

It also gave me the means of examining my prison more
closely and this I set about as soon as I was left alone,
though with little profit. There was plainly no escape by the
door, while the walls were solid stone, and the only hope I
could see was the timber partition on one side already
mentioned. Here the stonework was just shoulder high, and

the boarding above it about another arm's length, but heavy and nailed from the outside; and when I began to try it to find a weak place there was a voice beyond which growled, 'Let that be, now.' It sounded an ill-tempered fellow, and when I enquired softly how much a little assistance might be worth to him he answered, 'Nothing you can offer, you bloody spy; I'd as soon see you hang.'

'So ho,' I said, 'we have a somewhat serious situation here,' and after that there was nothing for it but patience and reflection; this being mainly concerned with where I had seen Mr Millichip before. Twelve years and more since, and it had been my chance remark of making a trick with every card they played which had brought it to mind. He was not one of my clients, but I had been attending the trial at the Old Bailey of a notorious highwayman I had taken on Hounslow Heath—who was later hanged with some cere-mony, and ladies throwing bunches of flowers to him—and I had stayed to watch the following case, which was attracting considerable interest and not a little fluttering of feminine hearts.

A cool, handsome, reckless young rascal known as Gentleman Johnny, who was reputed to have stripped even his prison warders by playing cards with them, and who had worked his way into the sporting county gentry. He was charged with carrying off a young woman, a minor, which she, her father and brother swore was forcible abduction, while he counter-claimed that on his part it was an honest elopement, and a put-up job because he had taken too much money off 'em over the gaming tables. Whatever the truth of it may have been, the judge had plainly taken a dislike to the said young woman and her father and brother, and given Johnny the benefit of the doubt; ten years in Botany Bay instead of a hanging. That would have brought him back to England about two years ago, I mused; plenty of time to settle down again, and now a man with more than enough experience to shoot a confederate who was threatening to peach on them and then trick an elderly and somewhat simple butler.

But there was little pleasure now in seeing how it was done, and less in reflecting that the rascals would get away with their plan unless I could somehow escape from this damnation hole. Except for intermittent bursts even the gunfire had stopped now, leaving that strange silence which seemed more foreboding than the rumble and thunder, and my patience was wearing thin by eight o'clock when they brought my supper in; bread and meat and, with further nice consideration, a jug of Belgian beer—a most uncommon cat piss and pepper brew. I had half contemplated another surprise rush, but the sight of three of 'em and a brace of pistols again persuaded me to caution; and on top of that there were two more blows to come.

The one in charge—a fellow with a wooden leg who had the bearing of a soldier—announced unkindly, 'There's a word for you from his grace. He says there ain't no such ladies known at the Hotel Bellevue, nor there's no messenger for you at the Suède neither. He says you'd best address yourself to your prayers, and don't try no more tricks.'

As our immortal Doctor Johnson has observed, "When a man knows he is to be hanged it concentrates his mind wonderfully", and I concentrated mine to find a better vintage than that unholy Belgian beer, selecting a fine Chambertin from the vineyard which they say Boney has his troops salute as they march past it. Then somewhat refreshed I approached the man behind the stable partition once more, now proposing ten sovereigns if he would only carry a message for me; and I shall not sully these pages with what he replied, except that it was discouraging. After that, about nine o'clock, there was a sudden commotion beyond, hurrying footsteps and raised voices, and I got my ear against the wood fast. My first thought was that Master Maggsy had arrived and bungled the matter from the outset, but from the sound of wheels and the clatter of hoofs it seemed that they were rolling out a carriage and putting the horses in; and another voice cried, 'Hurry yourselves now. Put the greys in for leaders. The ladies are leaving for Antwerp.'

That truly fetched me up all standing. There had been quiet talk of Antwerp at the ball last night, and this could only mean that the Prussians and our own troops were falling back; and as good as putting the rope round my neck, the rascals. I shall not rehearse the various emotions, philosophical reflections and other profane observations which crossed my mind in that last hour of ominous silence before I heard fresh voices in the stable.

This time is *was* Maggsy, thank God. I would recognise his dulcet tones anywhere, and he was playing 'em to the full. When I got my ear up against the partition again he was whining, 'Only looking for a horse for a lady, mister. She'll give a hundred golden sovereigns for a horse. The Frenchies are coming. Look there,' he cried, 'Godhelpus, ain't that one?' Hard on that there was a dull, horrid crack, and he muttered, 'Lay him down gentle, Jaggs; I hope you ain't corpussed him, they won't like it if you have,' and then hissed, 'Are you there, Sturrock?'

'By God, I am,' I said. 'And you've been long enough about getting here.'

'You count yourself lucky,' he snarled. 'Gimme that muck fork, Jaggs.'

The prongs of a fork then appeared in a crack of the woodwork, but there was also a fearful creak and some other fellow on guard in the passage bawled, 'What're you doing in there?'

'Saying my prayers,' I bawled back, at the same time whipping round to jam the chair they had brought me under the lock just as I heard the key turn. 'I've got a right to,' I yelled while there was a further splitting creak. 'He's breaking out, the bugger,' the man roared, shouting for help and thrusting against the door; while I bellowed, 'No, I ain't; if I'm to hang I want a parson! Fetch me a parson!' now banging with a wine bottle to add to the Hallelujah chorus and cover the noise Maggsy was making.

One board gone, and his face appearing like a demon from hell, one more breaking, but also three or four men in the passage putting all their weight on the door, forcing it a bit and starting to break the chair. One of 'em got his fingers round the edge, and I bawled afresh, 'Fetch me a parson!' administering a sharp crack with my bottle, which caused a yelp of agony. 'Fetch the Duke,' I yelled, leaning against the door myself as Jagger wrenched another board out, 'I'll make a full confession.' But it seemed the Duke had not waited to be fetched, for there was a sudden silence broken by whispering before he cried, 'What the devil are you doing, my man?'

'Why nothing, my lord,' I answered, now cursing the sudden quietness, one eye on Maggsy and Jagger straining at the next plank. 'Merely saying my prayers,' I cried. 'It's these rude fellows of yours who're making the noise. Send me a parson!' I bellowed as the timber broke away with a rending scream and Maggsy screeched, 'Come *on*!'

The Duke was quick but I was quicker. He cried, 'Have that door down!' I leapt for the opening; four of 'em fell in a heap on the floor; and the Duke stood ready behind with a cocked pistol. 'Gone away,' he cried, and fired.

It was an unkind shot, for he might have spoiled me for life. I swear that ball passed clean between my legs as I sprawled in the opening. I heard it smack on the stone and I felt the heat far too close to my Most Particulars, but then Maggsy and Jagger had me out on my elbows, and I was only reassured that I had those most precious possessions still with me when one poor fellow started through the opening after us and I found the strength to put my boot in his chaps to discourage him. It was an undignified business altogether, now with two or three horses kicking in their stalls and screaming, Jagger yelling, 'This way!' Maggsy cursing, and behind us the Duke roaring, 'Gone away! Round to the stableyard, men.'

I never knew so many ill-tempered servants in one household. As we got out to the yard ourselves there was a fresh gang debouching from a side doorway, the Duke with 'em, and plainly enjoying himself like a hunting man, crying, 'Tally ho! We'll have the scoundrels this time. Spread out, men, and shut the gates. Careful with your musket, Purvis; and give me that pistol.'

Thank God it was pretty dark. They couldn't just be sure where we were, and Maggsy muttered, 'Not bloody likely. I'm going; they'll gut us if we stop here. Jump for the wall, Jaggs, and give him a bunk up.' Then Maggsy scrambling like a cat, hissing 'Come on, then,' Jagger grunting, 'Hup she goes, now,' me somehow astride the coping without quite knowing how I got there, the Duke announcing,

'View, halloa; there they go,' a flash and bang—the musket this time by the sound of it—then another, and two more ugly smacks in the plaster. It was somewhat breathless.

Nor do I know how we reached the street unharmed and did not pause to wonder. Unlike the night before, when it was ablaze with lights, the rue de la Blanchisserie was now darkened for dread of the French coming, but there were fearful and curious people abroad, and what with the shots and the shouting behind us our hurrying footsteps on the cobbles caused fresh confusion; cries and questions, a woman screaming, 'They're here!' and one damned scoundrel even bawling, *'Vive l'Empereur!'* But they fell back from us as quick as we approached and in another minute or two we were safe amid the trees and the greater darkness of the park, where there was little chance of the Duke's men finding us.

There we slackened our headlong speed a bit; for which I was grateful, being somewhat fatigued. But I found the breath to say kindly. 'You've done well; though you left it late.'

'Couldn't do it before dark, could we? Maggsy demanded. 'We been nosing about that place all day since you never showed yourself this morning. Wasn't long before we got wind that they'd catched a spy meaning to assassingate Wellington. "This here's a rummy lot," I says, "but I'll lay odds that's Sturrock somehow". Then when there's a cove come from his grace the Duke of Richmond to ask does Mr Sturrock have a messenger from London, this about five o'clock, we're sure of it; specially as I hear this same cove tell the landlord to keep a sharp eye on me and Jagger as his grace might want us fetched along as well. I says, "It's time to get out of this lot, Jaggs", which we done by dropping the bags out of the window and dropping after 'em. We had to snout one of the menservants to do it,' he added. 'But nothing particular, and I reckon he was put to watch us anyway. So then I set out to find fresh lodgings for us, and Jagger come to see if he could discover where they'd got you.'

'That's right,' Jagger said, taking up the tale as we came out from the park into the darkened Place Royale. 'Let on I was a hired groom; brought a string of hosses out, got paid off and looking for a job but willing to buy a drink or two. Twas easy after that. The don't catch a spy every day and was willing enough to talk about you; a proper desperate rogue, they tell me. Got a good look about the stables, and they even showed me where you was.'

'You're a good man,' I told him. 'But where was Mr Millichip in all this; and what was he doing?'

'Well you may ask,' Maggsy answered darkly. 'Who knows where Mr Millichip is, or what Mr Millichip may be doing now? Mr Millichip's upped and disappeared himself,' he announced. 'And went last night, if you ask me. And what's more, there's been a big battle today, and they say Boney's licked everybody in sight. And if we've got any sense . . .'

'Be damned to Boney,' I cried; but after that have little further recollection. Even a man of my iron resolution may suffer a small weakness sometimes, and I felt myself stumbling and heard Jagger cry distantly, 'Hold up now.' Thereafter I had only an uncertain notion of them half carrying me down one dark street after another with Maggsy cursing and muttering, and saying, 'We're in a right mess if he's corpussed, Jaggs,' until at last he finished, 'Hold him up against the wall,' and set to knocking on something and calling, 'It's us, Mrs. Clancy.'

I came to this time with a taste of brandy in my mouth and a
strange vision of a lamplit parlour with Maggsy, Jagger and
several young ladies about. My first thought was of the
Duchess of Richmond's ball again, and that somehow I had
fallen foul of the cavalry captain after all; but I next
perceived that another of them was examining my sore skull.
A woman as big as the side of a house, of weather-beaten
visage and brawny arms, and speaking an Irish brogue you
could cut with a knife. 'Begod,' she announced, 'it's a fine
smack he got. I've seen 'em like this before. They'll walk for
hours with it sometimes, and then go out like a candle.'

'Not yet, ma'am,' said I, gathering my scattered wits, for
it was plain she was no heavenly visitation. 'Nor yet the
Duchess of Richmond,' I added fancifully, gazing round at
all of 'em in turn, Maggsy and Jagger and the four younger
ladies, and not so far gone that I could not catch the scent
and style of the place on the instant. 'It's a whore shop,' I
announced.

'Arrah, now, my man,' the woman retorted, 'keep a civil
tongue in yer head now if yer don't want another clout. A
gintleman's select lodging, if you plase. And Mrs Sarjint
Brigit Clancy. Me husband's Mr Sarjint Clancy of the First
Foot, the dayre crayture; and him and Ould Hookey as
close as brothers. Ye'll niver see nothing more rispictable
than that.'

'Ma'am,' I begged, blinking at her afresh, 'I ask your
pardon. But who's Old Hookey? And how the devil did I get
here?'

'The Duke,' she cried. 'Willington himself, you poor
ignorant soul.'

'You go easy,' Maggsy said. 'I done it. And couldn't have done better neither.'

'And indade he did and nor he couldn't,' she announced, slapping a cold compress on my bump with a force that damned nearly took my head off. 'I lit on him in the market lugging two great heavy bags and looking like an innocent lost lamb, the swayte ugly little monster.'

This fetched a guffaw from Jagger, but she continued, 'I was about expressing certain opinions on siveral matters, and he enquires, "Ma'am, are you English?" to which I reply, "Indade I'm not, thank God; don't be insulting, bhoy," whereupon he says, "You look all right to me, anyway; so can you say where to find a safe lodging for three of us in a bit of trouble?" ' She paused for breath on that, and then demanded, 'So tell me now, what have you been up to? Is it murder? I don't mind if it was a fair fight; but I won't have thayving. I'm bound to know if you're rispictable.'

'Ma'am,' I assured her, 'as respectable as you might wish for. We're out to settle the account for a murder; and to save two young women from more mischief than they've bargained for.'

She eyed me shrewdly, saying, 'No doubt there's more you might add, and maybe you will; but that chimes well enough with what the bhoy told me. By the same token there's room to spare on account of our regular gentlemen being away about other business.' And as if to give point to her words there was a sudden rumble of cannon again. 'That'll be Boney's twelve-pounders,' she observed. 'But they'll not trouble us tonight, and we'd best take a bite to eat now.'

I never saw the like in a whore shop before, certainly not in any of the establishments I am acquainted with in and around the Haymarket in London. A polite family supper with the young ladies of the nicest manner, though not otherwise having much to say for themselves, and now and again the menacing thunder of the guns while Mrs Clancy entertained us with tales of the war in Spain and all the way across France to Toulouse. For this remarkable woman made a regular profession of following the armies, as her mother had done in India before her, and she had been in Brussels since April when the forces here began to assemble. 'From Moore at Corunna to Ould Hookey at Talavera,' she said. 'It's comforts for the dayre souls. Did I not carry my own man on my back for twelve bloody, blistering, murdhering miles after he was shot in the leg at the storming of Badajoz? That was a fayrefull night, Mr Sturrock. When the dawn came, the ditch before that wicked fortress was smoking with blood. And Ould Hookey himself in tayres at the sight of it.'

We listened in respectful silence to these reminiscences and then to a further concussion of cannon which set the glasses rattling, and she announced, 'That'll be the Prussians taking it. The French don't commonly fire after dark unless they're punching home a victory. I've had my reports. And no doubt as quick or quicker than the high up gentry get theirs. There's a tale the other night that the Prussians sent the fattest man in their army with messages to Ould Hookey, and the poor bewildered soul took thirty hours to ride thirty miles,' she added, laughing heartily. 'But Boney fell on Blücher at Ligny today, against Ould Hookey's left flank while engaging our boys at Quatre Bras. The Prussians fought every foot of it, but they're in full retreat; and we're bound to fall back with them.'

'It's a serious matter, then.' I ventured.

'Betwixt and between,' she answered. 'There's many left for Antwerp in case of a sack, and as many more villains still here waiting to welcome Boney if he gets this far. But we mane to stay. My Mr Sergeant Clancy and Ould Hookey'll stop the rascal between them when they think the time's ripe. And then the dear man'll want to know where to come home to his supper when it's all done; for I've never failed him in a good meal after a battle yet.'

The guns were muttering once more, and I said, 'Ma'am, I take my hat off to you. I don't know which is the more fortunate; Sergeant Clancy with you, or the Duke of Wellington with Sergeant Clancy. By your leave, I'll tell our story now. And maybe even ask your help,' I added cunningly; for with her experience, I thought, she could well prove more useful than any other person in Brussels.

She listened as entranced as we had been by her own reminiscences, and when I had finished she observed, 'It's a queer tale.'

'Not as queer as it sounds,' I said. 'And simpler than it looked to start with. It's a tale of big money. But for me there's a murder to clear up. And I've a personal score to settle,' I added, fingering the side of my head.

'Aye,' she agreed. 'But speaking of money, Mr Sturrock..?'

'Say no more, ma'am,' I begged her, taking out Lady Dorothea's purse and laying it on the table. There was still some fifty pounds in it, a modest viaticum considering that after today's misunderstandings I could scarcely expect the Duke of Richmond to honour my letters of credit; but enough to interest the lady, I thought. 'I'm a businessman myself, ma'am. Take what you need,' I told her, though with some trepidation. 'We'll not haggle.'

'Aye,' she repeated thoughtfully, and then cried, 'Come

now, you girls, let's have this cleared away and think of our beds.' But when we were left alone to the sound of domestic bustle and laughter elsewhere—in which I noted Jagger and Master Maggsy were joining heartily—she asked, 'Now, my dear man, what is it you want?'

I explained at some length and she listened carefully, taking it all in, the good sensible woman. Then when I had finished she observed, 'It's a tall order. But there's scores or more of the ladies of the army in and about Brussels, though some of them are disreputable creatures. None the less, what they don't know isn't worth knowing. I don't hold much hope of finding your Major Finchingfield or Mr Millichip, but the rest should be easy enough. Even your damned black Protestant person.'

'He might tell us much if you find the right man,' I said. 'One who won't ask questions so long as he's paid.'

'Aren't they all like that?' she enquired. 'And speaking of payment . . .'

She reached out for the purse, and in sudden anguish I protested, 'What, ma'am? Not all of it?'

'It'll be an expinsive business,' she replied, 'and you offered we'd not haggle. I'm bound to see what you're worth.' So I was forced to sit and watch her counting out our money until she announced, 'I'll not strip you. Forty pounds.'

'No, by God,' I retorted. 'Ten. And that's generous.'

'Mr Sturrock,' says she sweetly. 'You know what to do if you don't like it. And a word or two to the Duke of Richmond would easily get you another lodging. But I've taken a fancy to you; and to your sweet ugly little monster. We'll say thirty.'

I know well enough when the other party has a half nelson on me. 'Thirty,' I agreed, only wishing to God I had the wicked bitch in London.

'Arrah, now,' she cried. 'There's a dear kind sensible man. And if you fancy a bit of company tonight to look after your poor head you're more than welcome.'

'No, ma'am,' I said hurriedly. 'I'm obliged, but no. I'd say my head had best look after itself, while I've still got that at least left to me.' And this was the night of Friday, June sixteen.

Eight

In spite of Mrs Clancy's perfidy and all our other perplexities I slept sound and woke late, only roused by one of the ladies bringing in a dish of coffee—a beverage I had never consumed at that hour of the day before—who informed me that all was quiet and a fine day though threatening thunder, and that Mrs Clancy had been out about our business since early morning. Then on descending to the parlour I was further reassured of the good woman by an excellent breakfast of yet more coffee, grilled ham steaks and uncommon little fresh baked bread rolls. And there I noted that the night hours of certain other persons had perhaps not been quite as quiet as my own, for Jagger had the look of a self-satisfied tomcat while Master Maggsy resembled a somewhat ruffled cock sparrow; avoiding my eye and flushing beetroot every time he caught the glance and the smothered giggles of the youngest of the young ladies who was serving us. 'So ho,' I said to myself; but made no other comment, for the boy was bound to get himself into something sooner or later and these girls were more amiable creatures than some of the London drabs.

This one indeed was a pretty little moppet, though she had all her senses about her in spite of the giggles, for she lost no time in giving us our instructions. 'You're not on any account to show yourself outside,' she said. 'Mother Clancy's caught word that the Duke of Richmond's having the town scoured for you. A French spy and two disp'rate villains who broke into his house last night.' She gave Maggsy another look and giggled again, but went on sensibly enough. 'And he'll have quiet all day and so'jers to do it with.'

'Quiet all day?' I enquired. 'What's happening, then?'

'They're getting ready for the battle,' she answered. 'That'll be tomorrow; or so everybody says. On a Sunday of all days. That Bonaparte's rale wicked, ain't he?'

With this we had to be content, waiting in the thunderous heat and a strange, brooding silence while I reflected that the absence of gunfire may sometimes seem more ominous than the rumble itself. But a bit after midday there was such a bustle and raised voices as could only betoken Mrs Clancy, and a minute later she entered pretty well propelling the one man I had known for several days must now appear in this affair. In short, a parson. 'There ain't so many of 'em,' she announced, 'and this yin's the one. One of our ladies knowed of him. The Rivirend Bleaker.'

I must say I did not take to the look of him. I like my parsons plump and rosy for a sign that they understand the ways of Providence, and this poor fellow was so cadaverous that he didn't impress me very much. Nevertheless I was at my most gentle and polite with him. 'Good day to you, sir,' I said. 'And we're obliged to you for coming. Mrs Clancy, may we have a glass of Madeira for the reverend gentleman and ourselves?'

'What is this?' he asked. 'And who are you? And where is this wounded soldier you said required my comfort?'

'Arrah, my dayre man,' she replied cheerfully, calling to the girls to bring the wine, 'that was a mayre blarney to fetch you along payceful. Mr Sturrock'll explain to you.'

'I will indeed, sir,' I interposed before he could protest again, now noting that Master Maggsy was horror-struck on tenterhooks. 'If you'll answer but a few simple questions you may help us prevent a grievous harm. And first, did you perform a marriage service during the late forenoon or the early afternoon of Thursday, June 15?'

This was a long shot—though fired from deep reflection on all the facts of the matter—but it reached its target, for he answered, 'I did; yes.'

'Thank you, sir.' Still careful and polite I bowed and continued. 'The bride being a Miss Georgina Wilde-Hookham, attended by another woman; the bridegroom an Ensign Thomas Debenham, and he probably also attended by a Captain ffoulkes?'

He gazed at me in some astonishment, but answered again, 'That is correct.'

'What it not somewhat irregular?' I next asked.

'It was,' the Reverend Bleaker confessed. 'I was in grave doubt about it. But the gentleman who arranged the matter, a Colonel Ashfield, the young lady's guardian, took me aside privately and explained . . .' He stopped here and looked sideways at Mrs Clancy. 'In view of the young lady's condition; and the possible mishaps of the imminent battle . . . For the sake of the child . . .'

'In the family way, was it, the poor crayture; and in case she's made a widder?' Mrs Clancy enquired as the wine was brought in. 'God bless ye, my dayre man, that's nothing new. It ain't the first drumhead wedding, nor won't be the last. I've seen dozens in me time.'

'Quite so,' I interposed. 'But this colonel, sir. Did you recognise his uniform? And was he a heavily built man, but not corpulent; a deeply tanned complexion and reddish moustache, with sharp blue eyes; and aged about forty?'

'I did not know the uniform,' the parson admitted. 'There are so many of them. But the rest suits the gentleman.'

'We're dong very well, sir,' I assured him, for he was growing ill-tempered. 'And there's only one more question. Did you take the service in church or in a private establishment?'

'In a private house,' he said. 'That, too, was irregular, but . . . What is this catechism?' he demanded.

'A matter of the law, sir,' I told him sternly. 'It was all too damned irregular by half. Come now, Mr Bleaker; the address.'

There are few can resist me when I put that manner on, and he said, 'A lodging house. Number Four rue de Flandres.' But he stopped then, eyeing me somewhat strangely, a sudden cunning look about him. 'Did I hear you addressed as Mr Sturrock?' he asked.

'No, he ain't,' Maggsy screeched. 'He's Lord Hookham. Lord Wilde-Hookham.'

'No doubt,' Mr Bleaker observed, still more cunning. 'And I'm honoured, my lord. But if you will permit me to withdraw . . .'

Too late I perceived what Mrs Clancy had done, as so did she, for she cried, 'Oh dayre God,' then adding, 'Whisht, yer Rivirence, where's the haste. Stay now and take a glass of wine.'

But the Reverend Bleaker was well on his high horse by now, and it was plain he meant mischief. 'I do not take wine,' he announced. 'Neither do I care for this place. Or the company here.'

'Don't ye, begod?' Mrs Clancy demanded, turning boiled beef about the face. The fool should have been warned but he was already too late, for she called, 'Girls!' and they were at the door before he had time to turn; when she said, 'We've a gintleman who don't much care for us, me dayres. I've a mind to tayche him better.'

'No,' he cried. 'Stand back from me, you shameless creatures.'

His voice went off in a scream as they fell on him. I would not have liked to tackle the four of 'em myself, and this poor ninny was helpless for all of his screeches, struggles and entreaties. The pretty dears took it as a playful frolic, and I fancy Master Maggsy and Jagger were half inclined to join in, but there was no need of it for those sprightly wenches had the man helpless before he could get a blessing out. A meagre parson was nothing to them after private soldiers of the British Army, and Mother Clancy said, 'Have him in the little room, now. We'll kaype him for a bit; but mind you trayte him nice.'

He was carried off backwards in a rush to the accompaniment of sundry bumping on the stairs, squeals, laughter and several surprising curses, and she continued, 'God forgive me for laying hands on the Cloth. But he's a poor crayture, for every prayching damnation. Will ye hear that?' she asked, as a fresh cry of anguish rose from above. 'They'll be having the pantaloons off him now.'

'Ma'am,' I said, 'I'm obliged to you. But I trust the reverend gentleman don't discommode you in the end. He looked spiteful to me.'

'Arrah,' she retorted, 'it's a pastime for the girls. And he'll niver dare spayke about it. He'll be laughed at spaychless if he does. None the less I'll be thankful to see you on your way. So listen now whiles I tell what I've found out for ye.'

'For the first,' she continued, 'there's niver sight nor scent of a messenger for ye at the Suède. But by what the ostler there tells me that's no wonder, for there's niver a horse nor conveyance to be had between this and Ostend. And what there may be the post keepers will not send into Brussels. For the next, two young craytures dressed as ensigns put down at the Bellevue but gave no names and were met by anither officer; a more elderly manner of man.'

'Major Finchingfield,' I announced. 'Alias Colonel Ashfield. Bound for the rue de Flandres; and we must go there after 'em.'

'Go aisy if ye do, then,' she warned us sharply. 'The Duke of Richmond's still seeking ye. And he's as good as the gov'mint here.'

'It's a chance we must take,' I told her. 'If we find these young women we shall find our Major Finchingfield and Millichip; and that'll clear the matter. I've got a score to settle with those fine gentlemen. But if we don't we must get to young Debenham somehow.'

The good woman nodded with evident satisfaction. 'Aye; well I've been at work on that for ye. The Fifty-Second Oxfords are standing at a place called Mont St Jean; so are the Tenth Hussars. They drew back there yisterday. And so is the First Foot and Mr Sarjint Clancy. He'll tell ye where to find 'em. It's a place about twelve miles out, beyont Soignes Forest, but there's supply train layving by the Namur Gate at four o'clock. The last waggon'll stop for ye. And it'll cost ye a sovereign to the driver.'

'Another sovereign?' I protested. 'Come, ma'am, this matter's getting expensive.'

'It's a small price for your neck,' she observed. 'You'll be best out of Brussels for a bit, my man. And by the same token I want ye well out of this house. Listen now, me dayre,' she wheedled. 'There's an *estaminet* called the Three Pigeons just ahint the gate. The rascal who kaypes it is a spy; he counts the troops and supplies passing out, but there's no rayle harm in him. If it playses you that way I'll be waiting there for you by four o'clock. If it don't you can take yourself and your baggage out of here and be off. And I'll let that poor snivelling parson go free to save meself further trouble.'

'Ma'am,' I said sourly, 'they should turn you loose on Bonaparte. You'd skin him alive.'

There was nothing for it but to agree with the avaricious bitch's terms, and we left our baggage with her—when no doubt she examined that to see what it was worth—taking only my powder, shot and pistols concealed about us. I had a notion that we might need 'em before long, and I was itching to get Major Finchingfield and Mr Millichip looking down their barrels. It was then two o'clock of a heavy, thunderous afternoon, the weather itself a portent of the coming battle, and the city strangely quiet as we made our way by the least populous lanes and alleys to Number Four, the rue de Flandres.

Here, too, the street was quiet, although there was still a bustle of officers and messengers about the Hotel de Flandres, but I posted Maggsy and Jagger on each side of Number Four to keep watch, and approached the house alone. It was a decent and respectable-looking building, as was the woman who opened the door to me; a retired housekeeper I judged, clad in black bombazine, a bit sharp featured and Frenchified, but agreeable enough and speaking pretty good English. I presented myself as Mr Henry Debenham, to which she answered, 'Madame Cambronne,' and admitted me to a little sitting-room; also most respectable and orderly. Here she gazed at me enquiringly, without speaking, until I explained my business—merely to offer my compliments to the new Mrs Debenham, Mr Debenham himself being my nephew, and to enquire whether I might be of any assistance to her in the present uncertain situation —when Madame Cambronne then expressed her own most profound regrets. 'But the young ladies have already left,' she said. 'For Antwerp. But only this morning.'

'And very wise,' I agreed, and further explained that I had hoped to be present at the wedding myself, but had been prevented by the exigencies of travel. It struck me that she was somewhat puzzled for a minute by this, though she continued that for her part she still could not approve of the irregularity of the affair, but since the Reverend Monsieur Bleaker had agreed to it and the Colonel Ashfield had made the arrangements it was clearly entirely respectable. The Colonel Ashfield was a person of extreme correctness, she said; and he had bespoken the rooms for the two young ladies more than a week ago. 'Please understand that I do not wish trouble out of this, monsieur,' she finished. 'I made it of the utmost clarity that I did not approve.'

'Why should there be any trouble, madame?' I enquired. 'You've been most obliging. It's a romantic affair. A trifle foolish perhaps, but in times like these we must give way to the young a bit. But tell me now; did not Colonel Ashfield bespeak a room also for another gentleman? Myself, in fact?'

'So,' she exclaimed. 'That is it. He did engage one more room. But when he arrived himself he informed me that this one was unable to come.'

She was looking at me more than a little wall-eyed by now, but I observed, 'Quite so, madame. As I told you, I was delayed. And I'll not detain you longer, save for one more question. Colonel Ashfield must be about his military duties by now, so who is attending the young ladies to Antwerp? And did they leave an address there?'

I fancied that this took her between wind and water, but once again she recovered quick. 'Colonel Ashfield sent his servant, and a chaise,' she answered shortly. 'And they did not leave an address. I did not ask. You will understand, monsieur . . . What is your expression? That I desired to wash my hands of it.'

Wishing to God I had her on my own ground, where I could use my authority, I said, 'Indeed I do, madame,' and on that the street-door bell jangled. This time the door was seemingly opened by a servant, for Madame Cambronne stood listening to a mutter of voices in the hall for a minute before murmuring, 'Your pardon, monsieur;' then going out herself and shutting this door firmly after her.

I was there in an instant with my ear tight up against it, but got little better than the same mutter; a man's voice, madame answering him, and his voice again; now raised on a tone of asking questions. Hard on this I heard Maggsy's whistle from the street, that being our signal agreed on, and I next crossed to the window to perceive him staring at the house, his face alight with excitement and gesticulating like a little ape, jerking with his thumb to come out, when he caught sight of me. Then, however, madame reappeared, standing with her back to the door and a vinegar smile on her face. 'Monsieur,' she announced, 'I have just learned that the ladies gave one of my maids their address. If you please to wait here I will send her to you.'

The look of the woman would have warned an infant, and I replied hurriedly, 'No, ma'am,' stepping hard back against the window; a flimsy affair hinged at the sides and

fastened in the middle. One backwards blow of my elbow
shattered the catch, and I said, 'My business calls me
elsewhere.'

I was over the still and out in the street on the instant,
with Maggsy and Jagger closing on me. One more instant
and we were down the nearest alley, while behind us
madame had got her head out of the window and was
bawling. 'French agents!' to the officers and redcoats about
the hotel. But the good woman was already too late, for there
was a regular labyrinth of lanes here, and it was the work of
only another minute to turn out of one and into the next; and
then Master Maggsy uttered but a single word. 'Millichip.'

'So ho,' I said, though not all that surprised. 'And it's
pretty certain that the girls are there as well,' I added.

'Are they, begod?' Jagger demanded. 'So that's it then.
We go and fetch 'em out.'

'We do not,' I answered. 'We've too much against us yet.
And when we do go in I want the whole lot of 'em together.
But you can go back, Maggsy. Nobody can catch you, and
well you know it,' I told him as he put up his inevitable
screech of protest. 'Watch for Millichip, and if he comes out
follow him. If he don't it's unfortunate; but see you leave
yourself time to come to the Three Pigeons *estaminet* by four
o'clock.'

It was a poor place, and the patron little better. He was
standing at the low window when we entered, plainly
counting the guns in a team of light horse artillery as it
rattled past, and there were half a dozen or so more of a like
kind seated at the rough tables and muttering together. I
noted three or four pistols and an old musket among 'em, and
even a French flag barely concealed in one corner; no doubt

ready to be thrust out when the moment came. They looked as if they would all have cut our throats for tuppence, but I gave the patron a cold stare and then said, *'Vive l'Empereur'*, which seemed to put a better face on matters; for he nodded and grunted, watching the last gun go past, and then turned back to the counter to produce a bottle of cognac and three glasses. For good measure I explained further that I meant to cross the British lines after dark, and the rascal nodded again; 'There will be rain later,' he said with satisfaction. 'Much rain. It will drown the damned English.'

After that they left us alone, while we sat in silence listening to their low-voiced conversation; and from what scraps I caught it was evident that they expected Bonaparte to be here by tomorrow night. Blücher's name was mentioned several times, and although their uncouth jabber was not all that easy to follow I gathered by degrees that the Prussians had been driven back some five miles from Wellington's left flank; which could well mean a quick victory for the French tomorrow. In short it was an uncommonly quandarious situation, and one of the very few occasions when I shall confess that I was uncertain how next to proceed. On one hand, if the French entered Brussels, I had little chance of getting those damned girls out, and less of apprehending Millichip and Finchingfield; while, on the other, if I went back now and forced my way into that house, I could well get myself, Jagger and Maggsy all arrested without doing anybody any good.

True, if I could produce the women they might go far towards proving me to the Duke of Richmond. But could I produce 'em quick enough, and how far would that determined imp of Satan, Miss Georgina Wilde-Hookham, assist me herself? She had been a more than willing accomplice all the way, and I had no means of knowing how far she yet realised her own true position. If I was correct in my reading of the plot—and I usually am—Finchingfield and Millichip would not make their next move before the battle was over, and until then it would be all too easy to persuade the little fool that I was sent only to drag her away from her lover. There was only one thing to do, I concluded. I must go out to Mont St Jean in fact instead of merely appearing to do so, as I first planned, find this other young fool, drive it into his thick head that they were both in danger, and frighten him into using his authority as her husband. It was uncertain, it would take too long, and it was too damned roundabout altogether; but it was the best I could do.

It was near enough four o'clock and I was in a fever of impatience by the time Maggsy appeared, pausing in the doorway, peering round the dark little hole to find us, and then sidling across to slip furtively on to the bench beside me. 'I don't much like the look of this lot,' he observed.

'No more do I,' I replied shortly. 'And the sooner we're out of here the better. So let's have your report, and be quick. Did you see Millichip?'

'I seen him all right,' he answered. 'God's whiskers, I seen him. And you wouldn't believe . . .' He glanced at me sideways and decided suddenly not to indulge in his usual poetics. 'He went straight back to Mother Clancy's.'

'What?' I demanded. 'Are you sure of that?'

'Dead sure of it,' Maggsy said. 'I got eyes in me head, ain't I? And that ain't the only thing I see neither,' he added, now grinning horribly at Jagger. 'I seen that Pretty Polly of yours as well. While I was watching for Millichip to come out of Number Four. She come to one of the upstairs windows and stood there looking down into the street.'

'I knew it,' I exclaimed. 'I was certain of it. Quick now; how did she seem? Agitated? Apprehensive? Was she trying to signal or get out?'

The monster shook his head. 'Nothing like it. Merry as a cricket. She was laughing and talking over her shoulder to somebody else I couldn't see. She waved to Millichip when he came out, and he signalled all right. Made a move with his head as if to say "Get back out of sight, you silly tit".'

'You watch your language, my lad,' Jagger advised him sharply. 'So why don't we just go and fetch 'em out, guv'nor?' he begged of me.

'I've told you,' I said. 'We might do more harm than good. It's all as I thought it must be, and they're safe enough for a bit. Come back to Millichip,' I told Maggsy.

He looked round the room uneasily, at the Belgians or Frenchies, or whatever they were, all watching us. 'There ain't a lot to come back to. He come out of Number Four in a hurry, went into the Hotel de Flandres, stopped there a minute or two, come out again still in a hurry, stopped again seemingly to ask somebody the way, and then to Mother Clancy's. That one called Maureen opened the door to him, and they exchanged a word or two, but I couldn't get close enough to hear what was said for fear of 'em seeing me, nor I couldn't be sure whether she knowed him or not. She lets him in, and I think time's getting on and I'd better skip. Which I done.'

'And whatever that may mean, it's no good to us,' I mused. 'But never trust a whore-shop keeper. As Doctor Samuel Johnson once observed, "Never accustom your mind to mingle virtue and vice. The woman's a whore, and there's an end on it". But she'll be here any minute now,' I continued, 'so you two get outside and keep watch for her. If she's with Millichip or any other men or redcoats, give your whistle and then make yourselves scarce and use your wits. I shall come out fighting if I have to.'

'Getting at it again, are you?' Maggsy enquired. 'Nobody can't never keep you quiet for long. Not that I like the smell of things all that much neither. And you keep your eye on this lot. They're worse than the Brown Bear mob by the look of 'em; and not so cheerful.'

Then left alone there was nothing for it but to wait in repose, though easing my pistols in my pockets—which is a damned unhandy way of carrying 'em. But before long I heard Mrs Sergeant Clancy's ringing tones raised outside, admonishing Maggsy on something and enquiring if I was within, and there was no whistle or other signal as she came in accompanied only by one of her girls, both of them carrying a bulging sack apiece. 'Good day, Monsieur Marcel,' she cried to the patron in astonishing French. 'Here's another supply train coming, and if it'll save you the trouble of counting there's six wagons to it. And there you are, dayre man,' she called to me. 'Come quick, will ye now; they'll not wait for ye.'

I went out with my fingers still on my pistol butts, but Maggsy was there muttering. 'She's on her own right enough,' and Jagger was hastening back from the last street corner as the train of canvas-covered wagons came rolling past. The last one lumbered to a halt as Mrs Clancy raised her thumb to the driver, but so far as I could see nobody about was taking much interest in us. 'Up ye get by the back, me dayres,' she said. 'and kaype out of sight. But if there's any quistions asked ye're a surgeon and his apprentice gitting to the front as best ye can.' She thrust the sacks in after us, adding, 'Ye'll not objet to carrying those to Mr

Sarjint Clancy. He'll thank ye for 'em so long as ye're careful of the bottles. And don't forgit to give the driver the soverign I promised him.'

So we were off to Waterloo, with perplexities before and behind, though with nothing following us; or not yet.

Nine

Of all my journeys I recollect none so tedious as that last twelve miles from Brussels on the sultry and threatening evening of Saturday, June 17, with a brassy sky and inky clouds building up overhead. A slow plod all the way, our driver saying nothing but smoking an evil, short clay pipe, and me hoping to God that the barrels we were sitting on were not gunpowder; frequent stops to pull aside and let trotting columns or faster traffic pass by, and one for half an hour or more when one of our wagons got stuck off the road; the gloom of an endless forest where we could see lanterns flashing among the trees by the roadside; and then the rain. And when it comes to rain these Frenchies and Belgians have got our Sceptred Isle beat by a length and a half. This fell out of the sky like all the buckets of heaven tipped over.

It was gone nine, and I was gone past speechless when we lumbered to a final stop. A straggling village, so far as I could see in the gathering dark and curtains of piss; a tall, domed church to one side, and on the other a row of cottages and buildings ablaze with lights; and here also torches and lanterns shifting outside, carriages, horsemen and messengers splashing through the flood. 'As far as we goes,' our speedy driver announced. 'This here's Waterloo. If you wants St Jean it's a bit better'n a mile ahead.'

'What?' Maggsy demanded shrilly. 'Walk it? Through this lot?'

'There's many thousands of better men nor you lying out in it tonight,' the driver told him.

This abashed the selfish little wretch, as well it should; and to tell the truth it silenced an observation I was about to make. But I had long since given up all hope of returning to Brussels before morning, and I enquired. 'Is there any hope of finding a lodging here?'

The good cheerful fellow laughed heartily. 'It's packed solid right to the pigeon cotes; church and all.' He jerked his thumb at the lanterns and horsemen outside what I now saw was the inn. 'You might try there if you like. That's Old Hookey's headquarters. He might take you in, though I doubt he will. No, guv'nor,' he added. 'You'll do better at St Jean. There's plenty of room there.'

As so often before in this pestilential affair there was nothing else for it, and kindly allowing Maggsy and Jagger to take some shelter from the elements by carrying Mrs Clancy's sacks—which Maggsy had long since discovered were packed with food and liquor—we set off into the murk. It was a fearsome journey, lit only by flashes of lightning; rain, wind and mud, now and again horsemen splashing past us, sometimes the glimmer of a smouldering fire or a lantern, and Maggsy's observations for a melodious solo to the orchestra of thunder. God only knows how long we endured it; for I lost count of time; but at length we came on several more lanterns bobbing in the darkness and our first stroke of fortune. It was a supply wagon sunk axle-deep in the mire, half perceived figures moving about it, a powerful aroma of rum, and a voice as Irish as Mother Clancy's saying softly, 'Quiet now, lads. We don't want no off'cers on us. Nor yet them rascals of Inniskillings or they'll murther us for this.'

Knowing the Tribe Clancy by now and the nature of army sergeants everywhere there was only one man it could be, though he uttered a lively curse when I called out to him, muttering. 'Whisht now, men,' holding up his lantern to view me, demanding, 'Who the divil are you?' and continuing, 'There's naught here but an old mislaid cart; and the driver running his legs off for fear he's in the French lines, the poor soul. And naught in it but a few old kegs of Holy Water.'

'By the smell of it you've got a miracle on your hands, then,' I observed. But what he had got his fingers on was a pistol; eyeing our sodden civilian clothes in the lamplight with some disfavour, and it was touch and go for a minute until I said, 'For God's sake, lead us to some sort of shelter. We've brought you goods from Mrs Brigit Clancy; and we've put ourselves to some trouble about 'em.'

That changed the tune on the instant, thank God; for he cried, 'Ah, the good woman. I sint her word that we'd had nothing to ate for near enough two days, and she's niver failed me yit. Step this way, gintlemen,' he added, pausing only to call softly over his shoulder. 'Roll thim other kegs into the wood, bhoys, so's you know where to find 'em again. And mind you watch for off'cers.'

Then, with a mess can of rum in one hand and his lantern in the other, he led the way uphill along that accursed road and then through a broken hedge into what seemed to be a field of shoulder-high corn or barley. I never saw such an astonishing sight as was revealed by his feeble light in the sheeting rain, for among the glistening stalks there were men everywhere lying in the mud with their heads on their knapsacks, and blankets rolled about themselves and their muskets. 'Tread aisy now,' the sergeant cautioned us. 'They won't thank you to wake 'em; and if they catch a scent of rum they'll be on my men down there like a swarm of wasps, the thayving rascals.'

I began to perceive now what the rude fellow at Waterloo had meant when he said there was plenty of room at St Jean, while Sergeant Clancy continued, 'It's a fine soft evening. And if it wasn't for the water and the hill before us you could see the French fires from here, if they're not put out by the wet.'

'Be damned to the French,' I said. 'Where can I find the Fifty-Second Oxfords?'

'Those country fellows, is it?' he asked. 'Oh, begod, you'll not find them tonight. They go to bed early. They're over there to the right somewhere; but leave it before tomorrow. Come in now and be welcome.'

He had stopped at a hollow under a wall and another hedge, a rude shelter of blankets stretched above, a small fire burning and five or six more men crouched over something bubbling in a blackened tin. 'A bit of old pigeon corn and some chicken bones that we came by to boil up,' he confided as Maggsy, Jagger and myself gazed in some surprise at this strange scene. 'Leave that slop and rubbish now,' he commanded, falling on the sacks we carried. 'Toss it out to those poor devils of Coldstreamers there. We've better for ourselves here. Begod,' he marvelled, 'a baked ham! And a brace of capons. Bread and pies. And, be damned,' he finished, 'fine French brandy with it. Boney himself'll not be feasting better tonight, boys. The good woman must've found a fortune for this lot.'

I restrained myself from observing sourly that indeed she had, and that it had come out of my pocket; and just as darkly I wondered what fresh surprises that same good woman might yet have in store for us.

We were to discover that at dawn, but for the present I was constrained to agree that there was little hope of finding the Fifty-Second Oxfords in the rain and darkness tonight and we joined Clancy and his men at their feast. Thereafter we addressed ourselves to sleep; or for me an uneasy doze punctuated by horrid dreams of the Reverend Mr Bleaker, Mrs Brigit Clancy shaking her tits in unholy merriment, the Duke of Richmond and his wooden-legged soldier-manservant dangling a hangman's noose in his hands, and all of them chasing me through clinging fields of barley with further soldiers springing up whichever way I turned. It came as a kindly relief when I was roused by the sound of bugles and Sergeant Clancy bellowing 'Rise and shine, ye rascals. Git them muskets clayned.'

The rain had stopped, but there was little other comfort. Mud and dripping water, a steamy mist over the fields, a sullen sky over all, and soldiers indeed springing up everywhere above the surrounding barley; or, rather, getting stiffly to their feet. Never have I beheld such a vast concourse of dirty, wet and weary men rising as it were from the earth, and I thought briefly that if Boney were to attack now God help all of us. But there was little time for such reflections, for somebody close by was now bawling, 'Clancy! You men there, where's Sergeant Clancy?' There was a young officer pushing through the barley, Clancy muttering, 'Holy Jaysus; it's the rum wagon. Rimimber now, bhoys, that was the Inniskillings, and we never see a smell of it.' But Maggsy said, 'God's tripes, they've got us this time.'

It was my dream come true. Not mother Clancy or the Duke of Richmond, nor yet the hangman's noose—or not so far—but certainly that damned parson, the wooden-legged servant and two others; and Peg-leg and the young officer were both carrying pistols as if they knew how to use 'em, while the Reverend Bleaker was plainly in a spiteful mood, for he cried. 'There stand the men. And Sturrock. A French agent.'

'Well enough,' says the officer. 'Shall I shoot him now and have done with it?' He was actually raising his pistol, and adding, 'Stand away there, you fellows' to Clancy and his men, when he stopped and demanded, 'Wait a minute, though. Didn't I see you at the Richmonds' ball the other night?'

'You did, sir,' I answered. 'And it's damned ungentlemanly to shoot a fellow guest. I demanded to be taken to the Duke.'

Without my messenger from London it was little better than a stay of execution, but it was better than a ball in my skull on the instant, and to my extreme gratification Peg-leg himself intervened. 'Beg your pardon, sir,' he said, 'but them's the Duke's orders as well. He's to be took back to Brussels, and these other rascals with him.'

'As you please,' the officer replied, adding pleasantly to me, 'So you'd best march, hadn't you?'

It was another quandarious predicament, and I could smell Master Maggsy plotting mischief. But the time was not ripe for that yet, and, affecting to be well beat, I promised humbly. 'We'll come quiet.'

So with a kindly farewell from Sergeant Clancy, who little knew what part his wicked wife had played in this, we were taken from the field in good order, slopping through the mud and barley and ranks of soldiers to the road; where the officer gave me a pleasant nod as one gentleman at a ball to another and, as I expected, went about his own business. I fancy he did not care for the parson all that much; and no more did I. And here, as I also expected, was a chaise some distance along the road.

Me, Maggsy and Jagger were now marching abreast in front, with the others so behind us, and I commenced a most contrite but improving discourse on repentance and justice, while we made about a hundred paces from the concourse of soldiers; most of 'em anyhow moving forward the other way. Then I reached a particular fine point on the Ever Seeing Eye of Providence and His Awful Retribution, with the parson uttering a heartfelt 'Amen', and stepped back hard on the miserable bugger's foot to cripple him. At the same time I hooked my other ankle round Peg-leg's wooden stump and threw him back on his arse, the pistol exploding harmlessly over my head. It was dangerous and somewhat unkind but I was in no mood for niceties, and the parson had scarcely got to the top note of his screech of agony before Maggsy turned on the other man with a wicked low punch that doubled him up, while Jagger, just as expeditiously, put out the last, lifting the fellow off his feet with an upper cut which he could not have seen coming.

It was all done in an instant, and damned risky; dodging through a group of cavalry amid curses and lashing hoofs, pushing past a gun team and lost in a file of wet and weary infantrymen. I shall never know how we escaped, except for good luck and the confusion we caused; nor did I stop to enquire. The chaise was by a cluster of cottages which I had not noted the night before, and here by the grace of God the road was clear save for a few more soldiers falling into platoon. There was a danger of muskets, I thought, but bawled. 'Messages for the Duke!' and they fell aside to let us through, though somewhat puzzled; but then we were on the chaise.

I have never been more grateful for that reckless devil Jagger's wild driving. There was a growing clamour behind us, and even a shot or two, but we got off with a clatter, in another minute into the forest and in one more scattering a fresh file of infantry to a chorus of curses and several further wild shots from some of the ill-tempered rascals. But we broke clear of them also with no harm done, and for the first time I was at leisure to offer up a short prayer although still without any very clear thought of what to do next; except that we must stop somewhere before we got to Waterloo village.

As the event happened we stopped a damned sight more suddenly than I could have wished for. Jagger was now driving like a Bedlamite, Maggsy screeching curses and laughing at the same time, and me holding on to everything. The madman very near scraped off our nearside wheel against a foundered supply wagon, pulled somehow round a bend, and fetched us straight into the path of a six-horse gun-team and limber coming up at a heavy trot. There was never a chance for either to stop, for they were to heavy and we were too fast. It looked like a fearful carnage to come, and what followed then is another thing I shall never be sure of. With main strength the maniac hauled us off on a deceptive clear patch under the trees, the horses plunged hock-deep into mire and we struck something unseen with a rending crash. I had a vision of Maggsy flying like an angel to one side, while the gun-team rattled past on the other, and then the wreckage of the chaise descended about my ears and all was silent; or at least until I got my breath back.

It was a pretty sight. The chaise on its side with one wheel smashed and a shaft broken, though the horses were miraculously unharmed; me sitting on the ground with the feeling that my backside had been driven hard up against my shoulder blades; and the idiot Jagger standing a-gazing down at Maggsy, who was lying as still as a dead dog—and looking not unlike one. It took me a minute or two to let off the various observations I felt it necessary to make; and then I added kindly, 'If you've broke his neck, Jagger, I'll break yours.'

But a spill from a chaise is nothing to a hardened little monster like that. When I came to examine him he seemed to be no more than stunned, and nothing broken; and our first need was to get as far away as we could from that wreckage, for the revengeful Reverend Bleaker would surely pass this way himself before long. So setting Jagger to release the horses and bring them with us as if we had ridden off on them, and me carrying Maggsy, we drew back some distance to a convenient thicket where we could lie concealed.

Then there was nothing more for it but to wait for Maggsy to come round, watch the road, and reckon out which way to move next; all being very nice points, for Maggsy showed no sign of coming to, the traffic on the road was thickening by the minute as the day wore on—more troops, guns, wagons and horsemen coming out from Brussels—and it was an hour or more before Mr Bleaker and his company appeared; none of 'em any too good-tempered and the reverend gentleman limping heavily and crying the entire Book of Lamentations when he caught sight of the chaise.

There was no sound of the battle yet—indeed except for the constant rumble from the road there was a strange oppressive silence over all—but some time after we perceived a few soldiers coming through the trees and away from the lines; unfamiliar uniforms, and moving stealthy; but not British, thank God, for we caught a word or two as some passed close by. 'Deserters.' I whispered. 'And it ain't started yet. That looks bad.'

'Too bloody bad by half,' Jagger muttered. 'I reckon we should get out of this ourselves. Give Maggsy a shake-up to wake him, get on them hosses, and ride for it.'

'Let him be,' I said sharply. 'When they're like that they're best left alone.'

The rascal was growing sulky; but I was getting more than a little impatient myself, and when after some further length he growled, 'The little bugger's gammoning; and we've had bad luck, so why don't we own we're beat?' It was too much.

'Beat?' I demanded. 'Who says we're beat? I've never been beat in my life yet, and I don't mean to start now.' As I spoke there was a sudden prolonged rattle of musketry fire, coming from somwhere beyond the woods on the far side of the road. It lasted for several minutes before it grew ragged and died away; and that decided me, for I am not a man to be challenged by his own coachman. I announced, 'I'm going to see what's doing. And, by God, I'll find this Tom Debenham one way or another. You can keep your eye on those horses, and wait here till I get back. And as for this little wretch,' I added, gazing at Maggsy's look of sleeping innocence more than suspiciously myself, 'Try cold water on him.'

You may consider that even for me it could be a tall order to find one man in a concourse of seventy thousand or more. To start with I found myself at a loss in that pestilential forest, as in order to avoid any further unfortunate encounters I resolved to keep to the trees for as long as possible. Clancy had said that the Oxfords were somewhere to the right, and I first got across the road only to find that the undergrowth on that side was pretty well impenetrable; and with yet more deserters already lurking in it. What with watching for these dangerous rascals, pushing along blind paths, and getting foxed by bugle calls which seemed to come from all directions, it was close on midday before I perceived sullen daylight between the trees and at the same time heard a band somewhere playing the 'Marseillaise' and a roar of cheering.

This was some distance off, carried on the sultry air, and it was followed soon after by the first dull concussion of cannon and then a crackle of musketry; as I learned later the opening shots of the desperate outpost battle which raged all day for the Château of Hougoumont. Could Ney and Prince Jérôme have taken that it would have laid open Wellington's right flank before the decisive drive to break his centre and open the way to Brussels; but it was held by Nassauers and Hanoverians and our own Coldstream Guards against one attack after another, until the woods, orchards and gardens were choked with dead and the buildings themselves mere flaming shells.

As I came out of the trees now, however, on to a convenient little grassy knoll with the rye and barley fields stretching away to either side, all I could perceive of this was a cloud of smoke hanging in the sluggish air, for the château was concealed in a fold of the ground at the foot of a sunken lane. But I could observe the whole of the British and Netherlands Armies deployed on the reverse side of a little ridge; ever a defensive tactic of Wellington. An all too thin red line of the same fellows I had seen rising wearily from the mud this morning, the cavalry sitting in more colourful squadrons with their horses tossing and pawing as if impatient to be released, the Duke of Wellington himself and his staff riding quietly along the lines, and our own concealed artillery now thundering in reply. And strangest of all the cannonballs; throwing up gouts of earth as they landed and then lobbing and bouncing on as slow and seemingly harmless as cricket—until you saw the dreadful havoc of this random hop and skip.

It was near enough three o'clock before I found Debenham at last, not above a mile past the place where I had emerged from the forest. The Fifty-Second had been held in reserve all morning, but were now ordered forward, when I was caught up in the movement as they advanced to take station and directed to him by a private soldier; who seemed much amused to see a somewhat dishevelled civilian marching with them. The order was given to form square, and he was standing beside his colour sergeant clutching the standard —no more than a tattered rag on its pole—in the midst of hell's pandemonium; the roar of our own shot passing overhead, the crash of bursting shrapnel, and close enough to the French gunners actually to see them sponging out and reloading their cannon. A fresh-faced boy trying his best not to be frightened; as I was myself and not ashamed to confess it. He was deafened I fancy, for at first he took no notice when I roared, 'Debenham!' but his sergeant demanded, 'Who are you, sir; and what d'you want here?'

'His young wife,' I shouted in the man's ear. 'In danger, I must talk to him.'

'No time for that now,' the sergeant answered. But he was a good fellow, for he jerked the boy's sleeve and bellowed, 'Pay attention, lad.'

Neither was there time for question and answer as I had hoped for. The devil's symphony rose to a fresh fury on both sides and then ceased suddenly, leaving a concussed silence until the ears attuned themselves to other sounds; the incessant rattle of musketry down the hill, the more distant rumble of artillery in front and to the left, and then the shouted command, 'Prepare to receive cavalry!' I was somewhat at a loss, for only God could tell what the next few minutes might hold for any of us; but I had a Providential inspiration. A boy in love must surely write a letter to his young wife on the eve of battle, and I cried, 'Letters! Have you any letters for your Georgina? She sent me to fetch them.'

His sergeant nodded. 'That's right. He were writing most of last night.' But then he broke off to add, 'Here they come. Hark to 'em!' It was not so much sound as a drumming vibration which seemed to shake the earth itself. The steady hoofbeats of countless horses, and he muttered, 'The cuirassiers. There'll be five or six thousand of 'em there.'

The field was shrouded with drifting smoke, but it rolled and lifted, while a brassy glare of sunlight pierced the clouds for a minute and fell on the massed ranks as they came up the hill at a slow trot, catching their pennants and glinting off their breastplates and helmets. They were like a great wave, which must overwhelm everything before it, dark below and tossing and glittering at its crest, but the sergeant said, 'Steady, lad. They're better'n the cannon fire. They can't do us any harm so long as the square don't break.'

'Your letters,' I repeated urgently, not so sure of that by the look of 'em, and this time Debenham himself nodded and thrust a packet into my hand as the command, 'Prepare to fire!' was given and our front ranks went on one knee to present their muskets while the rear stood shoulder to shoulder. 'Fifty paces,' the officer counted, 'forty; thirty; twenty; fire!' and as they had advanced like a wave so they fell like one, breaking and tossing in a confusion of animals and men, with the dreadful clatter of shot on armour and the screams of horses and wounded.

Yet they still came on through the smoke. Those behind rode over and through the fallen, now faced by a bristling wall of bayonets and stopped short by them, actually walking their mounts helplessly around the square and glaring face to face with our men for a time. They were all about us, yet there was still something more I wanted and I do not give up easy. 'The other letter!' I yelled in his ear. 'The one she sent you from London!' I saw his lips shape, 'What for?' as the sergeant said, 'For God's sake, git out of here!' but I cried, 'Listen, Debenham. Georgina wants it to make things right for you with her family!'

It was a lucky shot. He was gazing transfixed at the towering Frenchmen as if he had never seen anything like them before—and for that matter neither had I—but their trumpets were sounding the recall now; some were already retiring, and Debenham looked back at me, seeming at last to take in what I had said, and grinning suddenly. He put one more much folded scrap of paper into my hand just as another irate voice demanded. 'Who the devil are you, sir? Get from under our feet, blast your eyes,' and I was hustled off to the rear and thrust bodily from the line; when I lost no time about getting myself well out of the way under a hedge from behind which our artillery was firing again.

I learned afterwards that this was only the first of twelve such prodigal and fruitless charges, but did not stop then to wait for any more. My first concern now was to get back to Brussels as quick as I could, and I resolved that rather than risk losing myself in that damned forest again I would return to St Jean through the fields behind the lines; and in that lay near enough my undoing. But I hastened on amid sights enough to last a lifetime—not least the dreadful procession of wounded carried back in bloodstained blankets—and as I approached our centre the heavy French cannon fire there died away suddenly again; thus plainly heralding some fresh attack.

Here our defence was lying in the trampled rye, only four ranks deep and just below the crest of the ridge. Our cavalry was waiting massed on either side, already restless, with Wellington surveying the battle from a little mound close by; mounted on his favourite horse, Copenhagen, dressed in a plain blue frockcoat and white breeches, pale and thoughtful, but as calm as he had been at the Duchess of Richmond's ball. At the same time I heard the beat of approaching drums and perceived that there were several other gentlemen and a young boy, also civilians, standing on a supply wagon to get a better prospect. I should have known better, for I was approaching my own danger; but without a second thought or look I got up behind them to view this further spectacle myself.

It was as awesome as the cavalry attack. A solid body of men appearing through the smoke, marching shoulder to shoulder in phalanx and shouting, *'Vive l'Empereur,'* trumpets braying and drums beating the 'rum-dum, rum-dum,

rummadum, dummadum', of their *pas de charge*. They
advanced as if on parade, and one of the gentlemen said,
'D'Erlon's divisions. There must be eighteen thousand men,
By God, Boney means to break through this time.' One
other was watching through a telescope, and without lower-
ing the glass he answered, 'Then he's mistaken. He don't
understand the Beau's strategy. They're magnificent; but
it'll be slaughter, the poor devils. They're too close together;
they can't hear commands for the damned noise they're
making. And look at 'em now, as they come closer.'

I should have known that voice, but I was so transfixed
that I paid no heed to it. I had neither eyes nor ears for
anything else, for this was the invincible march which over
so many years had broken most of the armies of Europe. But
now, as they approached, you could see that the mud
underfoot was clogging their boots, that many were slipping
and stumbling in it, and that the stalks of rye were clinging
about their gaiters. Pace by pace they came up the slope to
the beat of their drums, while one of the gentlemen by me
began to count in a low voice; and then at a single command
our own lines rose as if the earth had been sown with
dragon's teeth. The crash of their muskets was drowned by
the roar of artillery, and the field was again veiled with
smoke. I caught but one glimpse of the fearful swathes cut by
canister shot, figures falling and dissolving in the mist, but
then after what seemed only a minute or two the firing once
more ceased as suddenly as it had begun, and our cavalry
swept *en masse* over the ridge; though, I must add, nothing
like so disciplined as the French cuirassiers had been.

I paused for a further minute, watching Wellington—who
seemed to be displeased with the impetuous cavalry charge,
for he was giving orders as if to fetch them back, with

trumpet calls already sounding—and only then did I perceive the company I was in among these gentlemen here. It
was the Duke of Richmond. And he was gazing at me with a
somewhat less than kindly look. He closed his telescope with
a snap and said simply, 'Arrest that man'; then adding to
me, 'and we'll have no tricks this time, sirrah. You might as
well know that my people took your two accomplices some
time since.'

Ten

It was a sorry meeting at the cottages of St Jean, where the surgeons were now busy about their bloody work. The Reverend Mr Bleaker as spiteful as ever, Peg-leg also still in an ill-temper, several other grooms, etc., and Maggsy and Jagger; both crestfallen and much the worse for wear. In the few hurried words I had with them I learned that our horses had been taken by deserters, and that then growing anxious about my prolonged absence they had set out to come and look for me, only to walk straight into the hands of the Reverend Bleaker, Peg-leg and three or four more men fetched from Waterloo. In short, a delicate situation, which Maggsy had further improved by grievously assaulting the parson; and now by the look on the reverend gentleman's face he was looking forward to seeing us hang. But at least we should get our transport back to Brussels, I reflected, as Richmond had his own carriage here, together with a four-wheeled phaeton and several spare horses.

Jagger and Maggsy were put into the phaeton—where by their expressions a pleasant journey was anticipated by all—and I was ordered into the carriage with Richmond and the boy; whom I now perceived must be one of the children, for as we rolled off, leaving the thunder of the battle behind, he asked. 'Why are we leaving so soon, Papa?' I fancied, perhaps mistakenly, that it was on the tip of his tongue to continue, 'Is it to hang this person?' had he not been too polite to put the question.

'Because Wellington advised me that if we remained much longer we might not be able to leave at all,' he answered. 'He considers that we may be more useful in Brussels than here. Men have been deserting all day and spreading alarm there.'

'Is the situation as bad as that, sir?' I ventured to enquire. 'Have not the French attacks been repulsed so far?'

'So far,' he agreed shortly. 'But Bonaparte outnumbers and outguns us, and he has not committed the quarter of his force yet. It may all hang on the Prussians. Blücher has promised to come, but nobody seems quite to know where he is.' He fell silent, as if angered with himself for talking so freely to me, gazing out of the window at the sorry traffic on the road beside us—mostly carts full of wounded, or some even lying over the backs of horses—but then demanded, 'Are you aware that Wellington was fired on this morning; and by elements of the Nassau troops?'*

I felt my dirty and crumpled neckcloth tighten about my throat, as it might have been a rope, but answered, 'No, sir, I am not.'

'I hope that may be true for your sake,' he observed. 'But what were you doing at the battle lines?'

I damned nearly told him that I had as much right there

*This was another curious incident of the battle. A battalion of Nassauers was lining an outlying hedge near Hougoumont. During the morning Wellington rode down there to check the defences personally and they panicked, thinking that an overwhelming French attack was imminent. The Duke rallied them, but as he was riding away, some opened fire on him; whether accidentally or deliberately is still uncertain.

as he, but common prudence and proper politeness to the nobility restrained me, and I answered instead, 'I was seeking a certain Ensign Thomas Debenham. To help account for one crime and prevent another. And I've letters of his here which will prove it.'

He looked at me somewhat curiously, but did not ask to see them and turned to watching the traffic again, for the road was crowded as we approached Waterloo village, even with some troops trying to clear it. Thus we were moving at little better than a walking pace, and I now noted that there was a horseman coming up beside us, cursing the confusion and trying to edge his way through. A fellow in a fearful condition; reeling in his saddle, plastered with mud, and one arm strapped to his chest in a bloodstained sling. But I recognised the mustachios at least, and cried, 'Captain ffoulkes!' It seemed like a heaven sent intervention. 'You remember me?' I demanded, 'Sturrock. At Lady Dorothea's salon.'

Half clinging to the coach, he peered at me uncertainly, but before he could reply Richmond interrupted, 'You are Hussars, are you not, sir? How did the cavalry go?'

'They went,' ffoulkes answered. 'An' that's just about it. They went too damn far. Run out of hand and never heard the recall; slap into the French guns an' got cut up.' He shook his head as if to clear it. 'F'r all practical purposes we ain't got no cavalry now.'

Richmond gazed at him cold and hard. 'And you are leaving the field?' he demanded. 'While you can still ride?'

'By God, I'm not!' ffoulkes retorted. 'What the devil do you take me for? I'd call you out for that, sir, if we'd time for it. Can't appear again in this state, can I? Got me quarters here, and going to get some clean togs.'

He made to spur his horse at an opening in the traffic, but I said, 'A moment, captain, if you please. Tell me now, when was it arranged for Miss Georgina Wilde-Hookham to travel with you to Harwich and Brussels; and by whom?'

'What the devil's that got to do with this damn mess?' he enquired.

'It will help Lady Dorothea,' I urged him. 'Cast your mind back, Captain ffoulkes. The day the French Fénelon was killed at Hanover Square.'

To tell the truth I was thinking more of helping myself by arousing Richmond's curiosity, and, thank God, ffoulkes answered, 'Be damned, I been thinking about that. 'Twas a deuced odd business. Sent a message by some valet fellow latish that same night. Didn't understand it and didn't like it, but what could I do? Ladies ask a favour of a gentleman, a gentleman's bound to say "Certainly". Said I'd wait for 'em at the King's Arms by one o'clock the next day.'

'What message?' I pressed him. 'Who sent it, and how was it passed? By word of mouth or a letter?'

'What's this all about?' the simpleton demanded. 'The fellow spoke his words holding his hat in his hands. Lady Dorothea begged the kindness. Would I escort Miss Georgina and her maid to Brussels? Plain as that.'

'And you went by some very unfrequented post houses?' I asked.

'Wouldn't even call 'em post houses,' he agreed impatiently. 'Miss Georgina said that was arranged too; and they certainly got horses easy enough. Didn't matter much to me, as I had my own string. But it was all confounded mysterious.'

He made to spur his horse on again, and the Duke was plainly growing just as impatient, but I said quickly, 'Let me ask only one more question, Captain ffoulkes. Did you see any sign of Major Finchingfield at any part of the journey? Or did Miss Georgina receive a message anywhere?'

'Finchingfield?' ffoulkes shook his head. 'Never a sight of him. Didn't know the man anyway. Never saw him before Lady Dorothea's tea-party. But there was a letter waiting for Miss Georgina at the Sloop in Harwich. And now, sir,' he added pleasantly, 'be damned to you and your catechisms. I've more important business to look after.'

On that he touched his shako to Richmond and worked his horse back into the traffic, while the Duke remarked. 'I trust all that served some purpose.'

'The best, sir,' I assured him. 'If it helps to persuade you that I am what I claim to be.'

'What you claim to be is one thing,' he observed. 'What you appear to be is a French agent. And a dangerous fellow at that.'

'My lord,' I told him, 'there's no question of assassinating Wellington. Nor Bonaparte; more's the pity. There never was. Those tales are merely part of a cunning and ingenious plot; which I'm engaged about breaking. Or would be if it weren't for all the hindrances put in my way. And if my messenger had only arrived from London I could prove it to you.'

'Ah, yes,' he mused. 'Your messenger from London.' He seemed to be listening to the gunfire, now rising to a fresh pitch of fury behind us, but he continued. 'Very well. Prove it without him, if you can. What is this plot?'

'It's quite clear,' I said. 'Simply to abduct Miss Georgina Wilde-Hookham, and thereafter hold her to ransom or blackmail from her family. For, if Bonaparte breaks through and takes Brussels, Millichip and Finchingfield will

threaten to produce evidence that she was involved in a
conspiracy against Bonaparte. While, if he's defeated,
they'll threaten other evidence of a similar conspiracy
against Wellington. Either way the family will pay. In the
first case because the girl would be in danger of her life, here
in Brussels. In the second because there's more than enough
mud to stick to the Hookhams. A few years back Lady
Dorothea was known to be a professed Bonapartist. I may
say that she's not now. But her husband, Mr Dashwood, is a
Parliamentary Whig; and less than three months ago the
Whigs were all in favour of peace with Bonaparte on any
terms. Some of 'em are still opposed to Wellington.'

Still listening to the guns the Duke considered this and
then nodded. 'There's little doubt that if Bonaparte does
enter Brussels our present government will fall overnight.'

'And if he don't,' I said, 'if Wellington does hold him, and
then even a hint of a tale like this gets into the newspapers
it'll damned near start a revolution in London. It'll look like
a Whiggish plot. Nobody in their senses will believe it, but
whenever did the mobs use their senses? They'll go mad.
And you'll note how the rascals implicated Lady Dorothea
with that simpleton ffoulkes. He'll be ready to swear it was
her ladyship who begged him to bring the girl to Brussels.
These rascals make use of every card as it falls. Their first
plan went wrong and they had to murder one man to keep
him quiet; but they very soon made another. They're after
big money, and the Hookhams will pay it.'

'Yes,' the Duke conceded. 'it's ingenious. But then so are
you; are you not?'

'Oh, for God's sake,' I cried, 'what do you take me for?
Your Grace, at some risk to myself I went out to the
battlefield today to find young Debenham and put certain

questions and warnings to him. As it happened, there was
no time for 'em, but I did get two letters. One from
Debenham to this fool of a girl, which for mere decency I
shall beg leave not to read; or not unless we have to. And the
other from the girl to him. I have not had time to look at this
one yet, but I'll make three guesses. First, that it contains
something damning; second, that it was brought out here by
the man who calls himself Finchingfield some time since,
and third, that the same Finchingfield now has a copy of it.
Have I your permission?' I enquired, somewhat sarcastic.

I did not wait for it, but took out the much folded and
finger-marked paper at once; and I was correct on all
counts, for it was dated June third and said: 'My dearest, all
is *now Arranged*. I shall come to Brussels on the fifteenth, to
Number Four, rue de Flandres. Dear old Slocoach will come
with me and is at last persuaded to perform the Ceremony. I
have promised him that dear Cousin Dot will not be angry
when she understands all, and that when I come into my
own inheritance he shall go to Rome and Athens for as long
as he pleases; which is his dearest dream. And there is also a
Great Secret which I shall not divulge yet. Except that we
shall come also with a Very Brave Man who is prepared to
lay down his own life if he must, *and there will not be a Battle* . . .'

There were several further lines of endearments which I
did not trouble to read, but tossed the letter to Richmond
with certain observations I shall not repeat here. 'You see
it?' I demanded. ' "Prepared to lay down his own life" and
"There will not be a battle". They've got evidence there,
whichever way the cat jumps. I wonder which of 'em told
her what to write through their go-between?'

It pleased His Grace to look at me with rather more
respect, I thought; as well he might. 'And this dear old

Slocoach?' he enquired. 'Who is he?'

'The Reverend Doctor Erasmus Slocombe,' I said. 'An even bigger fool than the girl. Competent to solemnise marriages, but couldn't do it in London under the Marriage Act of 1753; which forbids the clandestine marriage of minors. But that Act don't apply to foreign countries, and he could marry her in Brussels safe enough. That was the bait to get her here.'

The Duke nodded, and seemed about to put a further question, but at the minute there was a fresh commotion on the road behind; shouting and a clatter of horses coming up on us fast. We were well out of Waterloo village by now; save for the slow carts carrying the wounded it was not so crowded here, and the guns also had fallen briefly silent again although there was still a heavy rumble in the distance. 'What's this now?' asked the Duke, leaning out to look, as I did myself.

It was a rabble of men galloping hell for lick, and more racing on foot alongside 'em clinging to their stirrups, scattering among the carts and in another instant all about us. 'Belgians,' the Duke said with a single glance at their uniforms, and called out to one of them, 'What's this?'

'The French,' this man shouted back over his shoulder, 'they're coming,' and another paused by the carriage long enough to pant, 'They've taken Hougoumont, it's in flames; they've broken through the centre.'

Then the disorderly gaggle swept on, leaving both me and the Duke somewhat thoughtful. 'If Hougoumont has fallen . . .' he said. 'But I don't believe it. I'll believe it when I see British troops running.' As if to echo him the nearer cannon broke into a fresh fury once more, and he added, 'Those are our guns. But there'll be panic in Brussels, and we've six miles or more yet to go.' He put his head out of the window again, calling, 'Your best speed, if you please, Purvis,' and then added to me, 'Pray continue your story. It will at least wile away the journey.'

'I hope it may do more than that, sir,' I retorted sharply. But I told the whole tale again, as I had done that other afternoon in his study, though now in more detail, and he listened with one ear on me and the other on the gunfire. 'So there we have it,' I finished, nettled by his half attention. 'There never was a Captain Louis Fénelon. The man was a figment. The creation of an émigré named Joseph Coignet, who had attached himself to Lady Dorothea's household through Doctor Slocombe in the hope of extracting a pension from her. Her ladyship's generosity to the unfortunate is all too well known. And Coignet would have had no difficulty in sustaining the part. I suspect he was a minor actor, since he appears to have had certain dealings with an establishment known as Sims' Theatrical Agency.'

'Interesting,' his grace mused. 'And how did you come to hit on this?'

I was somewhat short. 'By the use of my wits, sir. Doctor Slocombe was writing a work on Bonaparte's Russian Campaign from the account of Captain Fénelon. I chanced to examine this work; and I also came upon a letter from a publisher refusing the offer of it, on the grounds that it did not contain anything which had not already been printed in the public newspapers. I reflected that surely a captain of the Twelfth Chasseurs, who claimed to have gone all through that campaign, should have had something more unusual to say.'

'And acute,' the Duke said. 'Uncommon acute. But you are growing a little testy, Mr Sturrock. Pray remember that

I still have to be satisfied. So why did they murder this supposed Captain Fénelon?'

I was growing more than testy. I was growing damned impatient. 'Because he was going to split on 'em. The game was getting too dangerous for him. He meant to set it all down for Lady Dorothea and then disappear. And he could be pretty certain that her ladyship would open the letter before Miss Georgina left the next day, as he also meant to leave a nonsensical rhyming code written in the little fool's hand. Her ladyship got that because I found it myself, but she never saw the letter since Millichip came in while he was writing it. Moreover, the fact that Millichip made his escape so quick and neat points to another accomplice. And there's only one other person that can be.'

'Ingenious,' the duke commented. 'And why did they remove the body from the mortuary?'

'Either to find that rhyming doggerel—which might have raised too much inquiry at the inquest—or for fear he'd be identified as Joseph Coignet. Both reasons I fancy. These are rascals who think of everything and think fast. Understand me, my lord,' I disclaimed modestly, 'I did not hit on this all at once. I had to piece it together bit by bit.'

'And it does you credit,' he observed. 'You tell an uncommon good tale. Indeed, were it not for the letter found on you the other day . . .'

'Come, Your Grace,' I made so bold as to interrupt. 'That was planted, and well you must see it. All Millichip or Finchingfield had to do was to recruit four suitable ruffians and watch for me to come out of your house.'

I might have added more but he said, 'Wait!' looking out of the carriage again. It was another horseman coming on from behind at a hard gallop, somewhat blown and a British

uniform this time, a minute later reining in beside us as
Richmond called, 'What's the news? We've heard that
Hougoumont's gone and the French are through the centre.'

'Lord, no,' the fellow cried, too damned cheerful by half,
touching his shako as he recognised the Duke and announcing, 'Hammond, sir, of the General's staff. Despatched to
Brussels with the latest reports. It's touch and go, but it ain't
as bad as that; or not yet. The centre's getting devilish thin,
but still holding. So's Hougoumont, though it's in flames
and the Third Foot fighting hand to hand there. Likewise
the Haye Sainte farm's been overrun and the Hanoverians
cut up. Nor we ain't got no cavalry left that you'd notice. But
we can hear the Prussian guns and that means Blücher's on
the way; though nobody knows how far off yet, nor how long
he'll take. It's sticky underfoot, y'see. And Boney ain't put in
his Old Guard so far.'

The Duke regarded him thoughtfully. 'Otherwise I presume everything is excellent. Very well, sir; ride on to
Brussels. See that as many people as possible hear your
report. All French attacks have been repulsed with heavy
losses, and the Prussians are now in action with us.'

Just as cheerful the young gentleman tipped his hat once
more, but before he could spur off again it was my turn to
cry. 'Wait! Do you still have men stationed in the city?' I
asked the Duke. 'I want a guard put on that house; Number
Four, rue de Flandres.'

'*You* want?' he demanded. 'Be damned, sir, how do you
come to give commands? We might have more important
work for men to do if there's a rising there. Which is very
possible.'

'My lord,' I said, 'if we don't stop this mischief at its
source we can't tell where it may end.' Thinking of Gedge's

drunken mutterings on the way to Harwich I added, 'There's already rumours afloat in London,' and addressed myself directly to the young officer. 'A dozen or so men back and front of the house. Just have 'em loitering there. We don't want any open action yet. They may let anybody go in, but stop people coming out. In particular, hold any carriage that may be seen about to leave. If they have to, let 'em say it's military advice; say the streets ain't safe owing to bands of deserters.'

He gazed from me to the Duke and back again with only the chinstrap of his shako holding his lower jaw on. Meanwhile I waited for the explosion, but greatly to my surprise His Grace only gave a sudden laugh. 'Begod,' he observed, 'one cannot but admire your impudence, sir.' Nevertheless he nodded to the officer. 'You may take that as an order. And hurry.'

But if that was a surprise His Grace had yet another in store, for when we were rolling on again he continued, 'I owe you some slight recompense, Mr Sturrock. But before I explain why, tell me how you came to light on the Reverend Mr Bleaker. He is a most respectable gentleman, though exceedingly ill-tempered at present. I cannot see his part in the matter at all.'

Reflecting that if he was riding with Master Maggsy and Jagger he was probably a good deal worse by this time, I said, 'They had to marry the girl to her Tom Debenham to keep her quiet for the few days before the battle. And since Lady Dorothea had prevented Doctor Slocombe from coming to do it they had to find another parson. It was merely a matter of discovering which one.'

'By means of Mrs Clancy,' he observed. 'A very well-known lady in Brussels. You keep some strange company,

Mr Sturrock.' He laughed again, seemingly enjoying a jest of his own. 'And you owe me something for several bottles of my wine, and grievous assault on some of my people. Your messenger arrived this morning and was sent straight to me. But we'll call it quits now. There were also further letters from Lady Dorothea Hookham-Dashwood; one of them for you.'

'Then perhaps, sir, you will let me see it,' I suggested stiffly. 'And my messenger's report.'

I shall not repeat the report here, for it merely confirmed all I already knew arising out of Burchall's investigations, but Lady Dorothea's letter had more to say. 'We are pleased to inform you that Masters is making a slow recovery, and is now able to talk a little,' she wrote. 'It seems that it was simply that horrid sight which set off his stroke, but he also adds something to the effect that he thinks he saw the morning room door closing behind some other person. Since my husband's valet, Millichip, chose to absent himself without leave or explanation on Tuesday night we can only assume who this other person must have been. What is worse, however, are most alarming rumours—which I dare not even write down here—said by Gedge and other members of our staff to be emanating from a tavern in Oxford Street. My husband is deeply concerned with the possible consequences if these are allowed to go unchecked, and I have written separately to Richmond urging him to give you every assistance to that end. We beg you to bring this distasteful and very dangerous matter to the quickest possible conclusion.'

'I hope that satisfies you, my lord,' I said. 'And, by God, quick it shall be. Though I'm sorry for Jagger.'

It must be quick indeed, or I shall have my publisher counting up the pages on his fingers. In short, as we approached the town there was evidence of mounting confusion. Fresh deserters yelling that the French were coming, the road half blocked with wagons, several overturned and surrounded by looters, some of the rascals daring to try and stop us to take our horses until I showed my pistols and our coachman laid about with his whip; Maggsy, Jagger and even Mr Bleaker fighting from the phaeton behind, and the Duke shouting out that the front was holding and the French defeated. 'Mr Sturrock,' says he, 'I fear I shall have to leave you to your own affairs. It's plain I shall be needed elsewhere.'

'It's very plain, my lord,' I agreed, now on the best of terms with the gentleman, for he had already handsomely given orders that Maggsy and Jagger were to be set free. 'Put us down by the Namur Gate.'

If anything the disorder was worse here as he left us, with his coachman lashing a way through. The clashing of churchbells and the distant rumble of guns; an ugly crowd milling about the *estaminet,* where there was the French flag hoisted and a copy of Bonaparte's before mentioned proclamation posted on the wall; more of the savages cursing and spitting at cartloads of our wounded, and women screaming back at 'em as they endeavoured to bring water or identify the poor souls. We cleared a way for these with my pistols; Maggsy and Jagger using their fists and boots, and even Mr Bleaker lending a useful hand. The last we saw of him he also was helping with the wounded.

It was easier as we got into the city however, though there were gangs roaming the streets and shouting for the Emperor, all the shops and most of the houses shuttered up, and more French flags and proclamations appearing; a few military on guard here and there, but all too few. 'If we don't get certain news soon there'll be trouble here by nightfall,' I said. 'But this makes it all the easier for us.' Then as we hastened on, and when you could hear yourself speak above the racket of the bells, I continued, 'Listen, Jagger; I mean to go into that house, and go in quick; and I'm bound to tell you that you might have an ugly shock.'

'Dunno that I shall,' Jagger answered doggedly. 'Me and Maggsy was reckoning it all out while's we was waiting for you in the forest this morning. I very near killed him over it.'

'Well, it's as plain as a boil on your backside, ain't it?' the wretch demanded. 'She had to be in it. I never did take to her anyhow. We never wanted her in Soho Square.'

'Be quiet,' I told him, for I was sorry for Jagger. Nevertheless I asked, 'That last minute or two in the peach house on Monday. She got you in a clinch. Was that it?'

'My oath, she did,' he muttered. 'I'd got me back to the house anyway, and she pulled my head down until I couldn't see daylight. I thought, "My eye, this is where I gets it all", and made the most of it, until she breaks away just as sudden and says, "No, you mustn't; and I must fly now." I swear I never thought no more of it, guv'nor.'

'Why should you?' I enquired, reflecting that the good fellow had never been all that bright in the head.

By this time we were turning into the rue de Flandres and that cheerful young officer had done his work well, for the street seemed to be thronged with redcoats; a guard about the hotel, seemingly against looting, and a dozen or so more opposite Number Four, which also was closed and shuttered. I wasted no time on discussions but approached the sergeant in charge and said simply, 'Have that door down.'

'Who the devil are you, sir?' the man demanded. 'I dunno why we're here even. Godstrewth, I can't do that without orders.'

'You've got 'em,' I told him, and even as I spoke one of the shutters opened and there was the crash of a pistol and the smack of a bullet in the wall too damned close to my head. 'And that's why you're here,' I added.

Thus encouraged they needed no further bidding, but poured across the street, as nothing so provokes a military man as being fired on without offence given. With a dozen hammering against it they had that down in a trice; though I noted that they stood aside politely to allow me to enter first. But there was no time for further courtesies, for it was dark in the hall. I just had time to descry the dim figure of Finchingfield waiting on a landing of the stairs before there was another flash and bang; this time the ball very nearly taking off my left ear, and raising irritated curses from the soldiers behind as I fired back myself, one Wogdon after the other. And more than enough for the major, for he was flung away from the banister as if the devil had plucked him back.

On that and a woman's scream from somewhere up there I said, 'Now, men,' and we went at a charge, gaining the landing without further incident. There were four doors here, the major half lying against one and bleeding profusely; but before I could pay any attention to him another opened and Mr Millichip appeared. Cool and steady, the rascal, and also with a pistol in each hand; one held on me, and the other pointing back into the room behind. 'Hold hard, Mr Sturrock,' says he. 'I can drop the girl first and you after.'

With my own armament discharged and Maggsy, Jagger and the soldiers all tight on my heels, there was little I could do, but I said testily, 'Don't be a fool. You're a dead man if you do. These fellows here are annoyed. I'm arresting Finchingfield, Polly Andrews and you—Gentleman Johnny, late of Botany Bay—on charges of murder, abduction and conspiracy.'

The rascal had the impudence to laugh at me. 'Finching-field?' he asked. 'You still don't know the lot, do you? His name's Cambronne.' There was a scream again from inside the room, and he gave an ugly jerk with his pistols, both of 'em cocked. 'Quick now,' he said. 'I can only hang once. But I'll go King's Evidence for a free pardon for me and Polly. I'll tell it all. It was Cambronne's plot anyway. He was a French agent with the émigrés in London.'

'Why, you bastard,' Finchingfield got out. I would never have expected it from the state he appeared to be in, nor had I seen in the darkness that he had another weapon. But he got himself on his elbow somehow and fired point blank. Millichip hung in the air for an instant before he fell, with one of his own pistols exploding. Then all was fresh confusion. Another scream from within; Madame Cambronne herself flying out and wailing, 'My husband,' my men surging forward, Maggsy getting underfoot, and me pushing past all of 'em into the room.

That was the end of it. There we had Mistress Polly Andrews crouching in a corner, half beside herself with terror; and Miss Georgina Wilde-Hookham—or Mrs Thomas Debenham—lying bound and gagged on the bed, but both alive and kicking; and flashing hell-fire from her eyes. It would have taken more than a mere pistol battle to quieten that lady. What I said to the spirited little fool while I was releasing her, and what she said to me in return when I finished, I shall not relate here; nor shall I repeat what

Jagger said to Miss Polly Andrews when we finally took her off to a safe lodging. But I was sorry for both of 'em.

There is little more to add, though for the sake of those who like to see everything clear I shall allow myself a few more pages. Millichip was killed on the instant, and Cambronne alias Finchingfield died a short time after. Georgina and Polly Andrews were removed separately from the rue de Flandres; and then it was gone nine o'clock before we heard honest English cheering in the streets and learned that the battle was finally won—though at a terrible cost—and Bonaparte bolting for Paris once more.

The next day the Duke of Richmond was too busy for me to trouble him, but I paid a visit to Mrs Clancy for a few words; though not too many or two strong, for like every other woman in Brussels she had her lodgings full of wounded. Here I learned that Mr Sergeant Clancy and Tom Debenham had both survived and were now marching with the army into France. Then on the day after the Duke found time to entertain me to a glass of Madeira in his study before my own return to London; when I said, 'The woman Andrews' confession and my messenger's report now make it all quite clear, Your Grace.'

'The plot was started inadvertently at Hanover Square by Miss Georgina herself,' I explained, 'when she expressed a wish to Andrews that someone might shoot Bonaparte. This was some time after Tom Debenham was sent off to join the armies. Millichip had been valet to Mr Dashwood for twelve months past, and it was he who introduced Joseph Coignet as Captain Fénelon to Doctor Slocombe and so to Lady Dorothea. I'm satisfied that apart from doting on Miss Georgina the doctor was completely innocent; and more than simple. So far Millichip and Coignet were merely after what they could get in the way of pickings, but they were acquaintances of Cambronne, alias Finchingfield, alias Ashfield, at a tavern know as the Hog in the Pound in Oxford Street—a rendezvous of the sporting fraternity and certain even less reputable persons—and when Andrews repeated Miss Georgina's remark to Millichip it was not long before they began to put their plan together; not more than three or four weeks ago.'

The Duke was kind enough to listen with rapt attention, and I continued, 'The first step was for Andrews to whisper to Miss Georgina about a secret plot to assassinate Bonaparte; and then to hint about a high-ranking British officer who was party to it, who was also sympathetic to her affair with Tom Debenham and who would make all the arrangements for her in Brussels if she chose to go out there with Doctor Slocombe to marry the boy. The romantic little fool swallowed it like an oyster; she even made up a fanciful code for them as part of the game, and there's no doubt they'd have used that against her too. As the copy of Bonaparte's proclamation—which we found in the Hanover Square coach—was passed to Slocombe. If the old idiot had ever got to Brussels that could have been used to implicate him and Miss Georgina as Bonapartists, and probably Lady Dorothea and Mr Dashwood as well. As I've said before, it didn't matter to our clever rascals how the battle turned; they'd got evidence they might use either way. A plot against Wellington on one hand and Bonaparte on the other, whoever was the victor; and the Hookhams would have paid anything. Millichip had promised to marry Andrews on the money they made out of it.'

'My blood runs cold at the thought of the repercussions;

especially on the report of an attempt to assissinate Wellington,' the Duke murmured. 'May I fill your glass again, Mr Sturrock?'

'Quite so, sir,' I said to both propositions. 'So we come to the events of yesterday week at Hanover Square, Cambronne, alias Finchingfield, came there to warn Millichip through Andrews that Coignet was about to split on them. Andrews swears she did not know that they were about to murder the fellow; and I'm inclined to believe her. Millichip fired the shot, and it was daring, but not all that risky. He was still regardᵤ¹ as a respectable servant in a respectable household, and all he had to do was to be seen in the hall innocently asking what had happened. Unfortunately, however, Masters the butler now appeared and Millichip was forced to make a hurried escape through the morning room. But here the luck was with them, since Polly Andrews was playing fast and loose with my own coachman and they were engaged about certain amatory exercises in the garden.'

I coughed on that, and took a sip of my Madeira. 'I need not go into details here, but in short my man swore quite truthfully that he had not seen anything; and at this point I myself had no reason to suspect Andrews either. Millichip then made his way to the Hog in the Pound, where Cambronne joined him a little later with the news that there was no danger from Masters, since the old man had been stricken speechless with a stroke. Here we now have the evidence of the landlord of this tavern, arrested in London on my instructions. He deposes that they next hired his carriage and engaged the services of two rascals known to be engaged in the resurrection trade, and there is no doubt that after removal from the mortuary the body was deposited at a hospital or medical school; as it would have been after the inquest in any case.'

I paused again to refresh myself, and then continued, 'Cambronne subsequently met me for supper, when I gave him to understand that I was satisfied the matter was a simple suicide, and he proposed that we should repair to the mortuary; ostensibly to search the body, but in fact to assure himself that it had indeed been removed. At this point he could not have known that their plans had received a further setback. Namely, that on my discovery of the rhyming doggerel in Miss Georgina's handwriting Lady Dorothea and Miss Harriet had extracted the plot from the young woman, and packed off Doctor Slocombe to the country. I may add that when I later discussed it with her ladyship she was exceedingly reticent about the matter.'

'Understandably so,' the Duke observed.

'Quite understandably so,' I agreed. 'And I did not press her. Miss Georgina, however, is a young lady of considerable determination; as you might have perceived yourself by now. She would not be put off, and through Polly Andrews again she had Millichip go to Captain ffoulkes' lodging and beg him to escort her to Brussels. Millichip had already returned to Hanover Square, and this errand was made all the easier by Lady Dorothea also instructing him to go to the House of Commons to advise Mr Dashwood that their carriage would not be waiting for him when the House rose at twelve o'clock.'

'Upon my soul,' His Grace remarked, 'it's difficult not to admire the clever villains. And you too, sir.'

'You are very kind, my lord,' I replied, savouring the rarest Madeira it has ever been my privilege to taste. 'And the rest of it is plain and simple. The two of 'em met the next morning to review the situation, and Cambronne then posted on to Harwich to wait there. Millichip was to follow that night, remaining in London I fancy to observe what I was up to. And then his greatest stroke of impudence was actually to travel with my party under pretence of being sent by Mr Dashwood; when he almost certainly sent a message on to Cambronne from the last post house, and contrived to delay us long enough to miss the girl.'

'Very clear,' the duke said. He glanced at me with something near a twinkle in his eye as he filled my glass once more. 'But what of your curious involvement with the redoubtable Mrs Clancy?'

'That, sir,' I explained somewhat stiffly, 'was fortuitous. My clerk happened on the woman by chance; and then I imagine that Cambronne and Millichip discovered that we were at her house from the inquiries she made about the city for me the next morning. She refused to tell Millichip where we were plainly because she was using us to carry certain goods out to her husband at the front, and she did not wish to spoil that errand. But she released the Reverend Bleaker late that night, and told him how to find us.'

'And he came straight to me,' His Grace finished. 'Quite excessively annoyed. We'll call that affair an unfortunate misunderstanding shall we, Mr Sturrock? And now, what do you mean to do with the woman Andrews?'

'As to that, sir,' I said, 'I don't fancy carrying a girl of that age back for trial and transportation, or worse; nor does my coachman. And I don't think Lady Dorothea would ask it either.' I savoured that beautiful wine again thoughtfully. 'I've taken the liberty of a word or two with Mrs Clancy. I'd say she's a woman who knows how to keep a wayward creature in check; and if it could be arranged to let Andrews be released quietly it would save several people much that they'd sooner not think about afterwards.'

'I daresay that might be done,' the Duke mused. 'And Miss Georgina? Or Mrs Thomas Debenham? I suppose she is, by the way?'

'There's no doubt of that,' I replied. 'She's married all right. As to Miss Georgina, I would say that her rightful place is with her husband; God help him. I understand that a number of ladies of the highest society here are preparing to follow the armies to Paris, and it shouldn't be too much out of the way to find a suitable chaperon for the little pest. I think I may engage to persuade Lady Dorothea and her family that it's a blessed release for all concerned.'

'Quite,' said His Grace feelingly.

'Quite so, sir,' said I.

So there we have it at last; except for a last word from Miss Georgina herself, received two weeks or so later from Paris: "Mr Sturrock," she wrote; "I still consider you to be a *Most Odious Man*: especially in giving the letter Tom sent to me to Cousin Dot instead. But I expect I must forgive you this also, and even admit it *very clever*, as she sent to say that she was *most deeply touched* by it and could do no less than wish us to be very happy. As indeed we are. You will be pleased to hear that the band of the Fifty-Second plays in the Champs-Élysées every day and all is a *Perfect Whirl of Gaiety*."